JOURNEY TO STORMREST
—CHRONICLES OF ALTIVA: BOOK ONE—

Airship 27 Productions

"Journey to Stormrest"
Chronicles of Altiva: Book One
© 2023 Teel James Glenn

Published by Airship 27 Productions
www.airship27.com
www.airship27hangar.com

Interior illustrations © 2023 Chris Nye
Cover illustration ©2023 Rob Davis

Editor: Ron Fortier
Associate Editor: Gordon Dymowski
Marketing and Promotions Manager: Michael Vance
Production Designer: Rob Davis

ISBN: 978-1-953589-48-4

Printed in the United States of America

10 9 8 7 6 5 4 3 2 1

JOURNEY TO STORMREST
—Chronicles of Altiva: Book One—

BY TEEL JAMES GLENN

Dedication:
To Jamie Ramos, a brother in words and soul.

And to ET who keeps surprising me and supporting me.
Thanks, both.

An Umbrian's Challenge

The Dark awakes and stares at me
The soundless terror speaks
The elder beings scream my name
And from the shadows creep
In nightmares and in dreams they crawl
Entwining in my soul
And yet I will not bend to them
To them I will not fall
My eyes I will not turn away
My head I will not bow
For in the north this man was reared
In mountains draped in snow
Beneath a steel blue sky
Where civilization dared not go
And anything that can harm my flesh
That might make another cry
Surely with my sword in hand
I'll cause to bleed and die
So beings dark and devils deep
This north born warrior fear
Born on a battlefield
Bred to the blade
No living nightmare
Can make me afraid!

CHAPTER ONE:
SUMMONS TO DEATH

The Shoutte of Shoutte looked out the window of his keep and was filled with dread. The mist-shrouded valley below and the brown, jagged hills beyond showed no movement—yet he knew that somewhere out there in the gathering darkness, as the two suns set, predators stirred and hunted.

"We are all predator or prey," he said aloud to the two people who stood behind him. "It is my duty as clan head to make sure we are not the latter."

The woman who stood behind him was clearly of the same stock as The Shoutte, tall and dark haired, though she was younger than him by more than a decade and her night-black hair was not streaked with grey as his was.

The other man, like the clan head, had clan scars on his left cheek that proclaimed his bloodline. He was broad and muscular with short-cropped hair and a full grey mustache, though with the same sky-blue eyes of the other two.

"Clan Kreill seek to make us subject to their svor thieving again this season," the mustached man said. "I say we should take action against them."

"The out guards are placed with the herds, brother," the young woman said. Her cheeks were unblemished by scars but had a tattoo in the same pattern as the men. "They know their business and will stay alert; I doubled them last week."

The Shoutte turned to look at the woman and his set features softened with the ghost of a smile. "You are my strong right arm, little sister; the clan owes you much, Cather."

"It is my inheritance too, Atrum," she said. "And I can see of late the burden is heavier for you."

The lord then looked to the mustached warrior and nodded. "And you, faithful uncle Kurvan, my eyes and ears among the warriors of the clan."

"I live to serve, Lord," the older warrior said. "As I did your father."

The clan leader acknowledged the warrior with a nod then his features hardened again. "Them damn Kreill," he said. "They harry me at every turn, even dealing with the hidebinders. Yet I dare not move against them directly; they have strong alliances with the minor clans and even the unaffiliated."

"They need to be slapped down …" Kurvan said.

"I know, I know, but if we move against them directly that wily she-tvek, Uta Kreill, will say we are against the accords and rally the clans against us." He shook himself as if to dispel a cloud. "No more talk now. I should finish these letters to go out tomorrow."

His sister stepped to him and kissed him on the forehead. "Endra is making avrum steaks and spice bread for supper. Don't be long."

"Spice bread?" He smiled. "I will rush these then; I shall have to be careful with my penmanship!"

"I agree with your sister, m'lord," the scarred warrior said. "Working yourself to exhaustion does no one any good."

The clan leader smiled and patted the warrior on the shoulder. "Next you will wet nurse me, Kurvan! But I promise to come down soon."

When the two had left, the clan leader locked the door and sat at his writing desk.

Despite his desire for the meal he wrote for more than a quarter hour until the twilight of the single sun slid into full darkness as the second one set.

As he put the quill down, however, he became aware that there was a strange shadow in front of him, not coming from the glowgems along the walls.

"By the Ancestors!" he whispered, as he turned. "What…"

Then Atrum Shoutte, Lord of Clan Shoutte tried to scream but no sound came out as a dark shape enveloped him in a smothering blackness. And before his heart could beat three more times, it was stopped forever and he was dead!

+++

"There are some obligations deeper than my wants, Arinna," the clerical student, Erique of Shoutte said. "I can not turn my back on them."

"I still don't understand why you have to go, Erique," seventeen-year-old Arinna Cabal said. "I know the message from the ko'ta bird said your brother died, but you said you and he were not very close." Her fingers kept up a constant tattoo on the sword guard while her body was almost rigid with tension.

The petite redheaded girl sat crossed legged on the sleeping pallet in Erique Shoutte's clerical cell in the two-brand student's quarters of the Academy Kova while he packed his few belongings into several saddlebags. Arinna wore leather breeches and jerkin and had her belted rapier across her lap. She tapped on the knuckle guard nervously.

Erique was well over six feet, with broad shoulders and black hair tied back in a braid that went all the way to his waist. "All I know is that my older brother is dead. I don't know exactly how. The ko'ta bird message was sent by my younger sister, Cather," Shoutte said. "Those birds only carry limited information, thought impressions more than anything, but it felt as if something was very wrong. The note on its leg only said he died abruptly and I must come."

"What can you do?" Arinna asked. "Besides sing one of the truth chants to aid his transition?"

Shoutte was stripped to the waist while he packed his few belongings, revealing two interlocking brands on the center of his chest. The brands marked him as a student at the Academy Kova who had completed the first six years of his training as a priest of the Kova—three years studying the singing of the scriptures (which could not be written down so that each voice changed them subtly) and three years as a healer. It meant he had only three more years of warrior training to be a full, triple-branded priest. The adding of the third interlocking brand would create the Omphast, symbol of the Kova to proclaim to all the world that he was a full warrior priest of his religion and protector of his peoples.

"I will sing for him, that I can do," Erique said with the calm certainty of the convinced but with deep sadness. "But there is another reason I have to go back and do it immediately."

"It will still take weeks by ship across the Straits of Brainard."

He paused folding a ceremonial robe and looked up at his friend. "She sent a crystal script so I can take a warp portal all the way to Westral City. If the time of the year is right I can perhaps be there as soon as a few days from now. The portals only work on the coast of my homeland, you know, so I will have to rent a vorn there for the ride the rest of the way up to Stormrest, our clan's hold."

"Oh, that really is urgent then?"

"The heir must sit vigil with the lord's body within the first moon cycle," Shoutte said. "So that the clan is not without leadership or it will be seen as a sign of weakness by the other clans."

"The heir?" She said, "You mean…"

"Yes," he said. "After the vigil, when I must sit with Atrum's body, I will be invested as The Shoutte of Shoutte."

She let her breath out in a sudden gasp. "You will be a lord?"

"Yes."

"You're not coming back to the Academy, are you?" Her voice broke into a sob and she hopped off the bed, sending her sword clattering to the floor as she crossed the small room to stand directly in front of her tall friend. "You aren't, are you?"

"I … I don't know." Shoutte towered above the girl. His normally upright, athletic form seemed to collapse in on himself and his head sagged. "I left the highlands of Umbria to enter the Academy against my father's wishes. His own brother, Uncle Etrar had done the same against his father's and it always angered my grandfather. It was seen to bring shame on the whole of the clan. The Kova as with other religions, is not much respected in my homeland. Yet growing up I much admired my uncle. When others saw me as weak or—or defective because of my speech problem he was a comfort and a guiding light to me."

"You've talked about him often," she said. "He died the very next year after you came here."

"Yes," Shoutte said. "And when later my father died as well so my brother Atrum ascended to The Shoutte of Shoutte. That was six years ago. From my sister's letters, Atrum has been a good steward of the clan in that time."

"But why do you have to go back to take over?" she asked. "You've so often told me tales of your homeland but they were like dream talker, children's tales to me. I … I never imagined you would return to it."

Arinna and Erique had become instant partners-in-crime the moment they met. She had been raised at the Academy Kova in Tolan, the capital city of the country of Cozen. They were on the northern continent of the world of Altiva and his far-off mountainous country on the southern continent had always been a like a dream realm to her.

"Arinna," he said quietly. "You know I want to serve the Kova, it is what has filled my heart and more than anything how I feel I can be of use to the world, but this is my blood family and I have a duty to the Clan Shoutte…"

"But what abut me? What will I do here without you to yell at me for fighting too much?"

She threw her arms around his waist and pressed her cheek into his chest.

He dropped his folding and hugged her back. "Easy, Arinna. I don't want to do this either; I really never thought about ever having to go back, but when I accepted the Kova I had to accept that the supreme principle of the universe is change. This is just another change I have to accept."

"No!" she said. "I worship the Goddess Yulin so I don't have to accept anything. She is the Goddess of hope and mercy. I need her mercy now to give me hope."

"I know," he said, pulling away from her and turning to his packing again to keep her from seeing him tear up. "But I have to go; obligations are obligations."

She turned without another word, picked up her fallen sword with an angry gesture and left him alone in his room.

The Umbrian clerical student started to call after her, but stopped himself. "I know," he said aloud to her under his breath. "I don't want to say goodbye to you either, my friend."

He sang a truth chant softly to calm himself as he finished packing. *"In The Kova's way I strive today, To far shores of my soul—To live and die without fear or lie; as in the ancestor's days of old."*

He thought about all the years he had been at the Academy Kova, all the friends he had made, and how he had been more accepted by these 'strangers' than by any in his clan in the highlands.

When the twelve-year-old boy had left the highlands of Umbria for his journey from the southern continent to the Academy he had only the vague notion that he wanted to be like his uncle, to perhaps find a place he felt more like he belonged than the place that had birthed him.

Etrar had been the only one who encouraged the sickly boy—had shown him exercises to strengthen himself, given him potions to deal with his lung sickness when the others in the clan would have let him languish. He had also given Erique his first instruction in how to overcome the severe stutter he had. It was the stutter that had been such a source of derision from his peers and the cause of a painful shyness in the boy.

The Umbrian Highlands were a place where the weak were not allowed, where the old dual god of the mountains, Zondra ruled with the dictum 'only the strong were worthy of breath.' Even the motto of the clan was 'Shoutte is Strength.' It was a hard place to grow for any but the most hardy, the strongest or the toughest.

Erique donned a simple cotton shirt and nekot fiber jerkin, belting it over his leather breeches with his straight saber, thinking about all the times he had belted on that sword since he had come to Tolan City and the school. Of all the classes, all the hours it had hung on his hip.

While there was a major concentration of each three-year phase, either to sing or to heal, every student studied the martial arts from day one as a way to instill discipline and to be able to defend their religion at any time. The Kova was not popular with many factions in the world and the adherents had often had to fight for their freedom to worship.

While the first brand was as a priest-singer and his second as a healer, it was only in the last three years where the martial arts were the paramount subject that would be studied. As a full triple-branded priest he would be the protector and law enforcer for the Kovar peoples of the realm.

Shoutte looked into the polished brass mirror on the wall of his simple student's cell. The face that looked back at him was a different one then when he first came to the Academy; not just older. Then he had no direction other than to escape the limbo of a second son, the continued clan squabbles and a life that was only about confrontation and death. He had very few warm memories of his homeland, something that he felt guilt about; after all, should not one recall joy when thinking of the place of their birth?

Erique had found purpose at the school, both in the depth of the teachings about the lore of the Kova, and when he learned his healing arts. It was only then that he knew deep, inner peace. The Academy was home now and he wanted no other.

"But blood is blood," he said aloud to the empty room as if to convince himself. "I must go back."

He left his room with his meager belongings in two saddlebags and a travel cloak draped over his arm. He walked slowly down the corridors of the student wing of the school, feeling as if his feet were weighted as he went to say goodbye to Arinna's father, Master Braphan.

Erique was stopped frequently by fellow students and a few instructors he met along the way for them to say goodbye and wish him well so that it took him some time. The normally reserved Shoutte was near tears several times along the walk. Since he had received the message two days before, word had leaked out that he was returning to his homeland to deal with the family tragedy. Most thought he would not come back.

In his heart he felt it as well and the thought of leaving was an open wound within him.

When he finally made his way out of the residence to the courtyard, Erique found himself looking for the little redhead who was his constant shadow for so long. Or was he hers?

The Academy Kova was on high ground in the center of the poor section of the capital city, a walled compound that had been an island before the dam was built to create what became the poor area, The Bottoms, all around it. The Academy was a center of learning and medicine for much of the northern continent and the training yard was the center of the Academy.

The training area of the school was divided into the quadrants where warrior classes were in progress, variously armed and unarmed in each quarter. Erique had spent many hours there over the years at the school in his minor studies, though if he were to continue he would spend the majority of his time there next. From the beginning it was the dictum of the Kova that one had to be alive to spread the word of the Supreme Principle of Eternal Change.

Arinna was usually in the yard by her father's side, for Master Braphan Cabal was the chief sword instructor of the school. Arinna was his most avid and most talented student, often teaching the beginner classes for him.

Erique stopped and watched the classes hoping to see her but it was one of the other instructors running the middle-level students through two-handed Iskarian Old Kingdom blade forms. It was a form that Erique favored, though Arinna thought he cheated by having longer arms to begin with when they fought.

The double suns—the larger blue Elder Brother and the small red Younger Brother—were at their zenith so there was no shade in the yard and the students sweated heavily, but with few complaints. At least none they would voice out loud.

Erique missed the certainty of hard training already, for he had looked forward to the three years to come. In the absolute energy of forms and combat matches he felt a strange comfort.

Those years will not happen. Not now, he thought and then he prayed to tamp down his anxiety. *To the Rythem, change is constant.*

He moved on to the corner of the courtyard where Reverend Master Braphon Cabal, as swordmaster-in-residence, had his office. The wide window of the Master's room gave an easy view of the training yard and the door to the room was always open to any student. Erique had spent many hours there seeking counsel from the older man, or apologizing for some mischief he and Arinna had gotten into.

This will be the hardest goodbye next to her, Erique thought.

The master was sitting at his desk attacking stacks of scrollwork with the same ferocity as when he used Wickcutter, his grown crystal sword in the training yard. The blade was in its carved crystal scabbard beside him at arm's reach. The sword had been grown around drops of his ever-freshened blood, bonding it to him in life and death. When he died it would shatter and, they said, that should it shatter he would die. There were not two hundred such crystal weapons on the world as most who even attempted to have one grown did not survive the process. That it existed was a mark of his skill and dedication to the way of the sword.

"Come in, Erique," the master said, without looking up. "No reason to cower outside the door. I know your step by now."

The Umbrian entered and, of habit, set his burdens down to take a seat across the desk from the master. "It is time to go, sir."

"I know," the master said. "Did you speak to Arinna?"

"Sort of. She is not at ease with this decision."

"Neither are you, Erique."

"I know. I should be, Master, but…"

"As much as we try to live by the Kova and accept all changes that come to us," Master Braphon said, "And all of us have a natural fear of change. It is why we study to be more perfect in our understanding."

"But I will miss you and her and all of this …"

"I know, boy," Braphon said, "and I will miss you, as well." He laughed. "I will have so much free time not having to explain away all the trouble you two get into to the other masters, I won't know what to do with myself."

Erique blushed and joined the master in a short laugh then sobered. "I will have to leave to make the warp timing, according to the warp wizard I consulted. The next opportunity for a warp portal to the south will not be for several weeks. I will not be able to look for Arinna to …"

"I gathered as much when she came running through here a little while ago," the master said. "She has been upset since you got your ko'ta message."

"I know, I wish I could make it … well … less painful for her. She does not have the Kova to comfort her."

"She is her mother's daughter in that," Master Braphon said. "She followed Yulin as well, but the Goddess gave her mother the hope and comfort she needed. And some times to give me the love and support I needed as well. It was not easy to be my life-partner, especially when I was a circuit cleric in the first years of our contract marriage."

"Will you tell her I will write, sir?" Erique asked. "As often as I can."

The master stood and stepped around the desk. Erique rose as the master put his hands on the young man's shoulders. "Erique, I could not be prouder of you if you were my own son. And you have been the brother Arinna has needed all these years. Losing her mother was a blow to her." His expression when mentioning his dead contract-wife brightened but there was still sadness in his eyes.

"I know you will make me proud no matter what happens when you get to Umbria, but I suspect you will not have time to write anyone for a while." His somber face lit in a sly smile. "So just to make sure, I think I will send someone with you to keep me informed of happenings there."

"What do you…"

"How long will that take on vornback from Westral City to your home in the mountains?" Arinna said when she stepped from the back room of the master's office. She was dressed in traveling leathers and had a backpack on. "You know I don't like riding very much."

Erique was stunned and looked from father to daughter with wide eyes and slack jaw. When he could finally speak, he only managed, "How can this…"

"Don't bother trying to talk her out of it," Master Braphon said. "She came to me yesterday with a plea to see you safely home and you know it is all but impossible to argue with her …" He put one hand on her shoulder and brought the two teenagers into a friendly embrace. "And you know is pointless to argue when the subject is reasonable anyway."

"But I have to take a warp portal," Erique said. "The expense …"

"Is not a factor," Master Braphon said. "The Academy has accounts with several of the warp wizards who provide passage and your other instructors agreed with me that a two-brand was too valuable to let go without supervision. After all, you will be a sort of ambassador for the Kova."

"Hear that?" Arinna said. "I'm supervising you."

"What?" Erique pulled away from his master to look down at the redhead.

"Not that kind of supervision," Master Braphon said with a chuckle. "But then you two always work things out when there is a problem."

The student cleric stared at his two friends for a long moment then burst out laughing. They soon joined him.

"But before you…" Erique began.

"I don't want to ride," she said, "so I was still hoping to talk you out of going."

"Just promise me you will keep her from ravaging your wild highland girls," Master Braphon said.

"I'm not sure if there are any Umbrian women that could resist her charms!"

"That's good to know." Arinna said with a grin. "But in the spirit of discovery I shall have to test your theory."

CHAPTER TWO:
WAY-STOP

"Come on and say that to my face, you tvekspoor!" Arinna Cabal said as she leapt up on the table with a wooden tankard in each hand. The petite redhead's eyes blazed green fire but her pretty features were set in a wide grin. "What, no stomach to say that to my face? Can't handle a real woman?"

The two men who had incurred the woman's wrath were both battle-scarred freebooters, still wearing their old shore-guard uniforms and still with more pride than prudence. The taller, shaven-headed sailor sneered at the angry girl.

"You wenches here in Westral should be honored to have a real man show interest in you!" He gave a derisive laugh but still showed respect for the tankards in the tiny teenager's hands as he stepped around the table she was standing on. His long-haired companion saw what he was doing and moved in the opposite direction to divide her attention.

"Please, little girl," the barrel-shaped barkeep of the tavern called from behind the bar. "Stop this before you break things and I have to deal with the city guard!"

The redhead laughed. "I'm not a little girl; I'm a full fledged woman," Arinna said. "The only thing I'll be breaking is the arm of this he-man who grabs uninterested females!"

At that the girl stepped backward, abruptly turning toward the circling bald attacker, which caused him to jump back. Then she jumped forward off the table to land with both her knees onto the chest of Longhair. Her sudden weight took the startled freebooter to the floor where she clapped the tankards together with his head between them. The sound was like a thunder drum from a temple service.

She rolled forward and spun to face Baldie who had recovered from his shock and drawn his short cutlass.

"You poxie slut!" The bald sailor advanced at her with a wild slash of his sword.

Arinna never bothered to make a move for her own rapier, dodging his sword easily, using one of the tankards to slap away the broad blade.

"Come on," she taunted. "Footwork, boy! My father wouldn't let you out of the beginner class with that clod stomping lumber!"

The freebooter slashed again and she nimbly danced away as he advanced, laughing until her foot hit an irregular board in the floor. The caught heel caused her to topple backward to the ground. The swordsman took advantage, lunging in to hack at her with his cutlass.

The redhead barely got the tankards up to punch into the descending blade, cursing as she did. "Bukrum's Belt!" she hissed.

"No one slaps me and lives. I will gut you, slag!" Baldie swore as his sword bit into the tankards. He pulled back taking the wooden cups out of her hands. He shook the sword to get the tankards off and this gave Arinna the chance to roll to her feet.

She backpedaled again, backing up to the bar, still laughing and deliberately still not drawing her rapier.

The other early morning patrons in the Westral tavern, a scattered half-dozen early drinkers, picked up their own tankards and backed to the wall, watching the fight that had come to them to enliven the day as it were a festival entertainment.

"Dame warrior, please," the barkeep pleaded. "Stop this or the guard will be on us and shut me down."

The redhead turned her attention from the swordsman long enough to shrug. "Sorry, but I don't like my butt grabbed, at least not by this tvek that passes as a man."

The barkeep shook his head. "You will ruin me." He then decided to appeal to the men, "Please, sirs, you scallywags, will get me thrown out of—Dame, look out!"

The warning was for another attack by the seaman but Arinna was already reacting, jumping aside as the man's sword blade hacked into the bar edge. She kicked out just below Baldie's lead knee, hard enough to buckle it, so he dropped to the floor with a curse.

She stepped in and slid behind the now kneeling man and locked her arms around his neck in a chokehold. The freebooter tried to pull her off, rising wither clinging to his back. He released his sword and clawed at her arms in an attempt to get her off him.

The redhead, however, had spent most of her life with a sword in her hand so her arms were like corded cables; they locked on the arteries on either side of his neck so that in less than a minute the man dropped unconscious, asleep. He even snored.

The patrons of the tavern broke out into applause. The redhead stepped back and took a bow.

"See, barkeep," she said, "only two tankards—no furniture damage at all." Arinna pulled a tollar out of her belt purse and tossed it to the bartender.

The barkeep already had a new tankard of ale for the grinning teen. "Yes, and a divot out of my bar that will be good for stories for a ten-day as this incident will become a tavern song to be sung of for a long time."

"I try to please," Arinna said. She drained half the cup and then wiped the foam from her mouth with a sleeve of her leather shirt then jerked a thumb toward the unconscious men. "Just not their sort."

The longhaired ruffian was moaning now, slowly coming awake.

"Want me to drag them up to the street?" Arinna asked.

The tavern was just below ground level on a back street in the poor section of the city near the harbor. The early midday crowd could be seen outside the window that was the main source of light in the room.

"Not worth it," the bartender said. "When they wake up they will buy some more beers to get over their headaches and stagger out, but I suggest you be gone by then or this will all start all over again."

"I'm waiting for a friend, I'm afraid. That was who the other tankard was for," Arinna said. "So I..."

"I'm here," a deep voice came from the entrance to the tavern. "And it looks like you started another party without me." Erique Shoutte stood in the doorway, his saddlebags over his shoulder and an exasperated look on his face.

"Not much of a party," Arinna said. She pointed at the two prone men, "These dance partners just don't have what it takes to keep a girl interested."

"I leave you alone for ten minutes while I get us lodging for the night and arrange vorns for the trip and you start a war?" He strode across the room to stand next to the redhead, towering above her so that she looked like a child next to him.

"That one grabbed my butt and called me cute!"

"How badly did you hurt them?" He knelt next to the fallen men and examined them with a healer's eye.

"Oh, no more than they deserved; I never even drew my sword."

"Yes, they'll live," he said. "Funny this never happens when I am around."

"Because morons like these think you're my boyfriend and don't want to cross a Kovar divinity student the size of a house."

THE REDHEAD STEPPED BACK AND TOOK A BOW.

"But you're still cute even when you're with me," he said with a grin.

She narrowed her eyes. "Don't call me…"

"I know," he said, holding his hands up in surrender then lowered his voice to add, "And don't mention the Kova around here; the locals are not very accepting of other religions beside the worship of Zondra. They especially are suspicious of the Kova."

She accepted his apology and said, "We should probably go somewhere else to have mid-meal before I get crankier for lack of food." The two of them went up the stairs with the inhabitants of the tavern giving Arinna one more cheer.

Once they were outside in the harsh sunslight they walked a short distance to a street stall where they got some plates of avrum steak, noodles, and some Juva ale.

While they ate the meal of the small, plump, and flightless bird, Arinna looked with interest at the hustle and bustle of the city, marveling at the cross section of cultures. She had not traveled far from Tolan and had little experience with the exotic mix the city presented.

The two friends had made the trip from the northern continent to the warp portal station outside the seaport town of Westral City in Umbria late that same morning. They had then walked to the waterfront, where they purchased supplies for the trip. They would have to head inland from the broad coastal plain and then up into the highlands.

"My body feels all out of sorts," she said as she shoveled food into her mouth at twice the rate he was eating.

"No one could tell it from how you are stuffing your face." He smiled as he sipped his ale.

"Ha, ha, giant," she said, between bites. "I mean it."

"I'm not surprised," he said. "That is a long warp distance from the north."

"What do you mean? I've been through a warp before."

"Your mind may not perceive anything when you step through a warp portal for a short distance," Erique said, now fully the student healer. "But your body knows you are not in the same place."

"But I've been through warps before," she said as she slurped some soup.

"But not more than twenty or thirty miles from the city," he said. "We have spanned what would have been a four-week sea voyage. The altitude, the different air pressures, the position on the globe, even the different pollen are things your body is recognizing. Sometimes even the water so far away can contain organism that make one sick till your body gets used to them."

"Good thing I drink this stuff, then," she said, taking another drink of ale. "This cheap swill will kill anything."

Around them the bustle of the active seaport town was a cross section of land lovers and seafarers from both the northern continent and the southern. There were even a few Mephan Empire traders in their silk finery among the leather and canvas trousers or slops wearing men of every class.

Arinna pointed out, however, that no one she had seen were wearing the highlander kilts. She asked, "Why is that?"

"Highlanders are not welcome in the city," he said, "nor are they comfortable here. They tend to stick to their own, feeling vulnerable out of the mountains and only come down in large groups to trade nekot or svor hides with the coastal traders."

"Is that why you are not wearing yours?"

He laughed. "In truth, I just have not unpacked it since my sister sent it to me last year. I had long outgrown the one I wore when I came to the Academy."

"Wait," she said as she finished her meal and gave a loud burp. "You have had a kilt a whole year and I didn't know?" She giggled. "I would have loved to see you wearing it with those long legs of yours."

"That is exactly why I didn't let you know," he said. He rose and took out some coins to pay the stall keeper. "You would have made fun of me."

"Only a little," she jibed then saw his expression was serious. "That's not the real reason, is it?"

"No," he said, "not all of it. I suppose I had not been sure how I feel about even being Umbrian at that point. It only reminded me that I had been an outcast here."

She put a hand on his arm. "I know you didn't talk about home much at first, then it was mostly vague history or about you and your sister and your uncle."

He nodded. "Yes, well, those were the good parts of it," he said. "By the time you knew me I had mostly gotten over my stutter but it was very bad when I was home. Only Uncle Etrar ever really listened to me and it was he who trained me in ways to overcome it."

The two of them were in the midst of the market along the docks now, the stalls full of trade goods from the northern continent, the far away islands of Mephan and Ker Nok as well as from the neighboring kingdoms of Avonia, Belise and Thorangia on the southern continent.

Arinna was used to the markets in her home city of Tolan but many of the fabrics and implements, especially some of the weapons in the stalls were strange and wondrous to her, a rainbow of colors and a garden of new scents.

She removed her languaring so that their whispered conversation in the Cozen language would not be understood, as she noticed few in the seaport seemed to wear the wizard-provided translation devices. Shoutte had already removed his as he felt it marked him as an outsider.

"I've never seen this kind of sword," she said, admiring a curved blade at one stall. The dark-skinned Amarian stallkeeper saw the light in her eyes when she looked at the sword and quickly stepped up. She looked down at Arinna's hand and when the redhead saw where she was looking slipped on her lingua-ring so she would understand the woman stall keeper.

"You have a keen eye, little warrior," the stall keeper said. The red-haired Arinna would have bristled but the Amarian was an attractive woman and so she gave the seller her best flirting smile in hopes of a discount. "That is a carved crystal Avook blade, a ceremonial weapon of my people who wiled it from vornback." The trades woman leaned in to expose some of her cleavage and ran a hand long the back of the smoky blue-colored weapon, sensing she could make a sale to the little warrior.

"Note the thick false edge," the seller said, her soft accent like a muted song. "It makes the blade almost as strong as a grown crystal sword. And the balance is perfect for a smaller warrior."

There was also incised script in the translucent crystal. It was in Old Mephan Kingdom script that Arinna could read with some effort.

"Thus the Nature of Zondra," she sounded out the written phrase. She looked up with a question in her expression.

"The dual nature of deity," Erique said. "In other words, it will bisect all it touches."

"Just so, tall pale one," the Amarian said. "You know the texts of the Dual One well."

Erique gave a laugh at that and nudged his friend. "Come on, Arinna, we have to get to the contract house where I got us a room before the day gets too far along. I left our gear there under lock before I found you at your little party."

"So soon?" Arinna said, splitting her longing attention between the curves of the blade and the seller who smiled back at her.

"We have to be up early," he said. When he saw his friend's longing look at the seller—and the seller's apparent interest in Arinna, he added, "So we don't have time for you to seduce any women and you don't have any money to buy a new sword. We want to be out of the city before the tradesmen swarm the town tomorrow morning."

"Seems a shame," she said, then when he arched an eyebrow added, "I mean, it is such a pretty sword."

He snorted and shook his head.

Neither friend noticed that when they through the seaport city their progress was followed by cold, dangerous eyes.

CHAPTER THREE:
RETURN TO YESTERDAY

The two friends walked for a while in silence, each lost in their own thoughts until, as they neared the Contract House of the Firehawk near twilight, Arinna spoke.

"So many tall buildings," she said, still amazed by the strange sights. There were more crystal buildings that rose to a towering three stories than she was used to seeing, even coming from the crowded Tolan in Cozen.

"The space is limited," Erique explained. "The coastal plain butts up against cliffs that are too hard to really excavate, so the city people build up on this strip; there is no other good anchorage along this coast for some distance. I also see that, since I left, they have begun to build structures out into the shallow waters to expand the city."

"And the cliffs are why we had to warp here?"

"Yes, those cliffs and the highlands beyond interfere with wizard-created warps," he said. "It is the reason Umbria was not successfully invaded by the Mephan Empire in my grandsire's time. The pass we will go through is the only way into the highlands." Then he added with pride, "That and great grandfather was able to unite the clans against the invasion; not an easy thing to get the clan to agree on anything but he bulled them into a confederation."

"Look!" Arinna said as they rounded a corner into the cul-de-sac where the Firehawk was located. What stopped her in her tracks was the red crystal building at the end of the street. It had elegantly sculpted angles that reflected back the fading light of the second, larger sun and seemed to spread liquid color across the ground before it. "What is that?"

"A Temple of Zondra," he said. "I had forgotten how lovely it can be."

"To the dual god?"

"Yes," he said. "Notice how the light from the prism spires split the light to blue and red, like the Younger and Older Brother, as symbol of the two aspects of the god."

"Temples to Yulin are so simple by comparison."

"Oh, it is simple on the inside," he said, memories washing over him. "Elegant in its simplicity, almost plain. A place to contemplate and be contrite."

"Can we go inside, or would it violate some custom?"

"No, all are welcome in the temple as in any religious sanctum." He pulled his belt tight to keep the wrap shirt closed with an obvious attempt to hide his chest brand.

"I thought you were proud of your religion," she said to him in a soft whisper while they approached the wide-open entrance to the sacred building.

"I am," he said, in the same Cozen dialect she spoke, "but no reason to start a holy war for no purpose. Even in the city they look with suspicion on out-country things, like any religion but Zondra. A relic of the Mephan invasion, really; the Empire worshiped the old taboo goddess, Ashun. So they mistrust out-country things." He made the sign of the Kova as if it was a talisman against the name of the ancient deity.

"Are you really so much different than when you came to the Academy?"

They stepped through the wide arch of the door into the vaulted interior of the temple and, as the clerical student had said, the space was simple and unadorned with wooden benches arranged along three sides. In the center of the space, lit by light from two skylights, was a pedestal with the dual symbol of Zondra surrounded by a reflective offering pool.

Erique almost made the blessing sign of the Kova before he stopped himself.

"I am afraid I am an out-country thing now," he whispered.

The two friends sat on a bench while Arinna soaked in the feeling of the temple.

Erique remembered sitting in that same temple with his Uncle Etrar the night before he took the ship to head north to the Academy Kovar.

"I'm f-frightened, Uncle," he said.

Etrar Shoutte was barrel-chested and shorter than his brother, Erique's father, but with a tremendous vitality that made him seem bigger. He sat beside the young Shoutte boy after the two of them had prayed to Zondra for a safe trip north for Erique.

"It is natural to feel fear, little warrior," Etrar said quietly. "Your war teacher, Dundak told you that. He says you have little enough of it in class, that you would fight rather than talk any day and all but fearlessly."

The boy blushed at the comment but it had always been easier for him to be physical than try to express himself with words. When his uncle saw his chagrin he continued.

"It is an instinct that keeps us alive, Erique, but fear can also motivate us to make easy decisions; not to venture, not to ask a pretty boy or girl for their hand, not to follow our heart because our head can find so much to be afraid of. Mostly, it is a fear of change that holds us back. And change is the Kova. It is the Supreme Principle. All things change, none can stop aging, or the rise of the suns or a full belly becoming empty with time"—he laughed, a deep, full laugh that was Erique's warmest memory of the older Shoutte—"so acknowledge the fear and embrace the change. You will do fine at the Academy. You will make friends and find the support you have not had here at home from the rest of the clan. Always be brave—never lose the fear, but never let it stop you embracing change."

"May Zondra bless you." A priestess of the dual god startled Erique from his memories. She was a woman of middle age, dark hair streaked with grey who stepped up to the two friends.

"And you, Reverend Mother," Erique said.

"You are not regulars here, my children," she observed.

"I have not been here for a long time," he said. "My friend had never seen a temple to Zondra, she is from the northern continent."

This made the older woman smile. "And how do you like it, little sister?" the priestess asked.

Arinna blushed at being asked to comment but returned the woman's smile with a genuine one of her own. "It is lovely, Reverend, so … so very peaceful here."

"Yes," the priestess said. "Our order has our quarters out back and many of our brother and sister priests stop here to renew themselves when they visit the city. Here is a place of peace to rest for the war that is life. You are visiting our city?"

"I have come home after a long time away," Erique said.

"For a visit?" the Priestess asked.

"For good, I think," he said with a dark whisper. "For good."

+++

"That sounded awfully final," Arinna said as she and Erique left the Temple after dropping an offering into the central fountain for luck. "What you said to the priestess."

The two walked across the *cul de sac* to the contract house. It was an unassuming building with the cutout sign in the shape of the feared flying Firehawk over the Ovar wood door beneath which was the Omphast symbol, discreetly smaller.

"I can't see how it is not, Arinna. I am here and I must come to terms with that. So, I am afraid, must you."

"You said you were not sure. That you were coming back to see." There was desperation in her tone.

"I said I was not sure how I felt, Arinna, but I do not see any way I can not assume the clan leader position. I want to continue with my studies, but ..."

The two friends knocked on the door that was opened by a smiling, older man. He had a long white beard but a young smile. "Good afternoon, gentles," he said. "Welcome to the Contract House of the Firehawk. Do you wish contract with a boy or a girl, or perhaps both?"

"Neither this night, good host," Erique said, formally. "I made arrangement earlier with Sister Gradax for a room and left certain articles for safe keeping. I am Erique of Shoutte."

The host never lost his smile but there was no recognition in his eyes. Before he could speak again a female voice called, "I will attend the gentles, Uvalt," she said. A small, plump woman came into the foyer of the building wearing a deep green down with an Omphast on it.

"Welcome back, Erique of Shoutte," the woman said to a grinning Erique. "Greetings, dame..."

"Arinna," the redhead said with a nod and a smile.

"Dame Arinna. I am Gradax, proprietress here." The woman, who was not much taller than the young girl waved them in. "I have your room in the back, and before you ask, it is still locked."

"I had no doubt, Sister Gradax," Erique said. "But as they say, 'Trust in Zondra but tie up your vorn.'"

This brought a laugh from the woman. "Just so, good sir, just so."

Arinna walked behind the other two looking into the main parlor of the contract house where, like the Kovar contract houses in Tolan, men and woman lounged while waiting to be hired for intimacy with visitors.

"I didn't realize there were any Kovar here at all," Arinna said. "At least from what I heard."

"Oh, there are not very many of us," Gradax said, when the group arrived at the door to the room Erique had rented. "We do not even have a full Priest-Singer, only some Priest-writers like myself for the city."

"I thought the Kovar were not popular around here?" Arinna said before she remembered she was speaking to a stranger.

"So we function more as a conventional brothel," the woman said, not showing any offense at all for the redhead's statement. "At least for those who do not adhere to the Omphast Covenent to fulfill their love contracts."

The Kovar did not have life marriage, in keeping with the principle that things change, but it was recognized that people form real and lasting attachments. So to balance this reality Kovar could contract with a partner in yearlong increments. It was required that before re-contracting for the next year each partner must spend a night with a different person. It was not required that they consummate the arrangement, but the very idea meant that the Kovar marriages were known to be most faithful because there was no pressure to fidelity or failure.

"Sister Gradax was just an intern at this house when my uncle and I stayed here before I left for the Academy," Erique said. "It is why I knew of this place."

"You've filled out quite a bit since you left, Erique," the proprietress said with gentle flirtation in her tone as she poked his muscular chest.

"So have you," he joked and she poked him in the belly and smiled.

"Just like Etrar, that rude, wonderful man." She giggled like a schoolgirl then her expression darkened. "I do miss him."

"I too," Erique said. "Each and every day."

The door to the room had a translucent box hooked to a bar on the door. The clerical student took a deep breath then sang several notes at it. The musical tones activated the crystal cylinders, and in a moment the sound lock opened and the door swung in.

"It is good to see his considerable faith in you was well founded, Erique," the proprietress said, her voice thickening and she reached up to touch his cheek. "He would be proud of the man you have become." Then she turned and hurried away just a bit too quickly to cover her emotion.

CHAPTER FOUR:
A LOOK FORWARD?

The two friends stored their gear, washed and changed from their traveling clothes to be comfortable before they ate supper in the kitchen out back of the contract house with some of the staff. The staff was a pleasant group; though most were not Kovar they were not hostile to the religion. Erique was more at ease than he had been at mid-meal if only for the fact that he did not have to fear their censure.

Gradax proved a jovial hostess and she had reminiscences of Etrar Shoutte that made Erique laugh and Arinna understand a little more how the older Shoutte had influenced him.

Several of the girls were not much older that Arinna and the two young men were of his age, though the men were more interested in chatting with each other than engaging the newcomers.

The girls were equally split with chatting with the tall handsome clerical student and Arinna whose warrior manner fascinated them.

"You actually teach swords?" A dark haired girl named Mozda asked. She had rushed to sit at Arinna's right and looked with a little awe at the play of muscles in the redhead's right forearm as she sliced some svor meat. "That seems so violent for such slight thing."

"And she's a mean teacher, too," Erique said. It brought a stern look from her and giggles from several of the girls.

"Somebody has to keep big goons in line," Arinna stuffed the svor undelicately in her mouth. "And they respect a prodding."

"Oh we have our ways of keeping big fellas in line," a dark skinned Amarian girl snickered. She had appropriated a seat on Erique's left side and was pointedly not admiring his forearms. "And a good prodding has a lot to do with it."

The table lost it in giggles again and the clerical student blushed. Arinna spit out food because she laughed so hard.

"You are all just too cruel on these weary travelers," Gradax said in an attempt to gain control of the jolly chaos. "They just want a meal and some rest."

"Oh, it's all right, Gradax," Erique said. "Everyone could use a little light entertainment."

"But they come from so far away," the Amarian said. "And such exotic a place as Cozen."

This remark made Arinna laugh. "Hear that, Erique, exotic?"

"Every where that is not home is exotic," he countered. "But they are speaking of you, mighty mite of mayhem. I'm home grown here in Umbria."

She made a snarling sound that startled Mozda which caused Erique to return the laugh.

"But if you're an Unbrian Highlander," a third girl at the table, a slender blonde asked, "how come you don't have a cheek brand?"

Arinna and Erique exchanged a suddenly guarded look and he was at a loss how to answer the question which could bring their mission to the fore but the Proprietress stepped in with a gentle dismissal.

"Oh, Eliras," Gradax said. "You know we don't get personal here at the Firehawk."

The blonde pouted but a fourth girl spoke up, clearly the oldest of the women. "I think that is a little deceiving, Gradax," she said. "What we do is…"

"No need to spell it out, Voltz" the Proprietress said.

Now it was Mozda that came to the verbal rescue to turn the course of the conversation. "We know, Proprietress," she offered, "but I can read the knowing cubes and they will tell us all we need to now about these fascinating strangers…"

A chorus of "yes, yes!" went up around the table, with even the two male sex workers who had been ignoring the conversation joined in the cheer.

Gradax looked exasperated.

"Yes," Arinna prompted. "I've never had The Tarrow Cubes read for me."

Erique arched an eyebrow and shot her a look but as usual she ignored his warning while the dishes were cleared away the dark haired Mozda ran off to her room to fetch the fortune telling stones.

"You don't have to put up with this, Erique," Gradax whispered to the clerical student.

"There is no offense, dear lady," he said. "A little bit of levity will calm down my little warrior friend. I hope."

The girl returned and removed a scarf she had been wearing to lay it out on the table. It was a cloth silk printed image of two interlocking circles in blue and yellow that overlap for a small sector.

"That looks like a Yoni Stone field," Arinna said.

"The Yoni Stones they say may be the origin of them," Mozda said.

"You've never had the 'cubes read?" Erique said incredulously to his friend. He sat down next to her.

"No," she said as if he should know. "No one in the Bottoms I knew does it; just the Yoni Stones." The Yoni stones were one white, one black and one grey that were cast in a circle

Mozda produced a leather cup, with an Ovar wood bottom. "This is an old set," the girl deckared proudly showing off the forty images on the ten cubes—carved from sea worm bone—with two blank sides on each cube. "Real Old Kingdom stuff!"

She dropped the cubes on the table, spread off the silk diagram. Everyone leaned in the moved the cubes back and forth to look at the images that represented states of being, experiences and personal connections. The Lovers, The Swordswoman, The Sacred Fool, The Crimson Saint, The Fansav etc.

"What do I do?" Arinna asked, bouncing up and down in her seat as if eager for a sword match.

"Well," Mozda assumed a serious instructor tone, "first you scoop them up, put them in the cup, give it a shake while you think of your future—hope, fears, worries—and then spill them out. Where they fall on the circles—how close they are to each other and the direction they face will tell us your future."

"Should I?" Arinna asked Erique.

He laughed. "You've never ask permission for anything before. Go ahead and see if you can find our when you'll get your next growth spurt."

She stuck her tongue out at him, picked up the cup and shook it.

"Think hard," Mozda said, then added with meaning—"See your desires before you."

The others giggled, even Gradax, who got into the spirit of the all with the Proprietress handing out cup of the good wine for everyone.

"Here it goes," Arinna said. "And—now!" After a few shakes she took her hand off the top of the cup then spilled out the cubes on the cloth. The small cubes rolled to a stop with many of them overshooting the two interlocking circles but with some within that overlapping small sector.

Mozda did her best to look serious as she surveyed the images and their positions.

"The position of the cubes in the sectors determine how the image influences the caster," she said in a hushed tone. "And these are—unusual."

Arinna shot a concerned look to Erique. "What do you mean—unusual?" The redhead asked. "Is that bad?"

Mozda paused for dramatic effect while all around sipped their wine and leaned in.

"There is The Priest, The Singer, The Sacred Fool, The Queen of Tankards, The Manor House, The Brothers, The Fansav, and Burdens. All these fall in spaces on the twin spheres that pertain to your future and wants." She read out the names of all the top images of the cube, as well as there was one cube with a blank side on top.

"We can see them," Voltz said. "What do they mean, oh expert?"

The dark haired girl all but hissed at the older woman but gave a sigh and began to decipher.

"Well," she said. "The Sacred Fool signifies you…"

"Wait,' Arinna protested, "Not the Queen of Tankards or something…" Erique stifled a chuckle.

"The Queen is quick to love or hate and is a fiery wench and a refined lady all at once." Voltz threw out as if in hopes to get a rise out of the red haired stranger.

"It's not what you think," Mozda said to forestall any upset, "The fool is the child heroine who experiences life in the moment and is ready for the world to amaze them. It is just the cube that approximates your position in the scheme of the future to come."

"That's better," Arinna agreed.

"It can be a dangerous position to be in yet no fear accompanies this cube and they may go where the 'brave' will not and gain greatness without really trying."

The redhead beamed at Erique who just rolled his eyes.

"But there is a strange thing here," Mozda continued, "the Singer and the Priest are in conjunction and cast a shadow on this Fool. And they must contend with the Fansav for the Manor House."

Arinna looked to her friend. "That's good, right?"

"The Priest—he is the path to the spirit using intellect, a positive cube, but with the caveat that to be caught up in the form of things can be misleading. And the Singer—as the Kovar say from up north, a song can heal, bring strong emotions. But to see them both together is not a usual thing."

Arinna cast a look to Erique and it was clear to him that she was afraid that their—particularly his—secret had been revealed. For while some might think him a Kovar to find out he was a Priest Singer could be great troubles for them both.

"I guess we don't need to know anymore," Arinna said in a attempt to stop the course of things, but the others shushed her with Voltz adding, "Afraid, little one?" Which brought a spark to her eyes that Erique had to quench with a look.

"The Manor House..." Mozda continued, "was a stable structure but see where it is in a flames, perhaps from external attack or from disaster within. And yet the Fansav—demons of the Kovar Religion agitate for the status quo; they do not like change and enjoy to be in conjunction with the ensnared cube. These forces are in contention and signifies that change, drastic and disruptive has or is about to occur. It can be good change or bad."

"I was just hoping to find out if I would meet someone tall and dark and curvy," Arinna said with almost a whimper. Erique looked to her with a concerned expression, regretting that she had begun the reading but seeing no way to end it without saying too much.

"You may still," Mozda said with a subtext, "Or at least someone dark and curvy."

"Finish with her, so I can go next," Eliaris said, "What do the last two mean?"

"Alright," Mozda finished, "The Brothers are obvious—one large..." She looked to Erique, "...and one smaller—which signifies the need for or the actuality for guidance. And Burdens—they must be assumed. They can be given or taken on; they can be obligations or inherited troubles all of which must be dealt with."

She sat back as if exhausted, flashing a seductive smile at Arinna. "Does that help you, red warrior?"

Arinna didn't know how to react, looking to Erique and a little uncomfortable, for she realized how close so much of the reading had struck to home. "Uh- yes, that was fun."

"Yes," Erique added. "Thank you, dame, for the reading, but unfortunately we need to head to bed early—we have an early start in the morning."

"Perhaps..." Arinna began.

"Bed and sleep," Erique said clearly noting the disappointment on Mozda and Arinna's faces.

"I guess so," the redhead admitted. She reached over and kissed the dark haired cube caster with just a bit more gratitude than a simple thank you.

"Good night all," he said to everyone at the table, especially Gradax. "This has been a pleasant break in our journey."

"...SOMEONE TALL, DARK AND CURVY..."

CHAPTER FIVE:
NO REST FOR THE WEARY

The two friends returned to their room intending to retire early, though Erique had to all but pull Arinna away from flirting further with the dark haired Mozda and Eliaris, who it seemed was also in contention for her attentions.

"You are insatiable," the clerical student said when the two friends were in their room again. Erique was already sitting on the raised sleeping pallet and unlacing his boots.

"I can't help it that I have what the ladies want," she grinned. "And they have what I want." She took off her own clothes, setting her rapier by her sleeping pallet to be quick at hand as was her want and wrapped herself with a travel cloak in liu of bothering with a nightshirt. The two friends had long passed any embarrassment or modesty.

"You know the taller of those ladies thought you were something special as well." She climbed under her covers and pulled them up to her chin. "The older blonde, Voltz, I think, who was trying to get me angry. And I know the Amarian was slathering for you."

"What?" He was naked and carefully set out the kilt his sister had sent to him, having decided to wear it in the morning and for the ride out of the city, if only to ease himself back into what would be his new reality. It was a red and black pattern with the feathered dragon that was the clan symbol woven into the fabric. It was heavier than cotton and made from nekot plants, one of the principle exports of the highlands.

"She was practically drooling over your long legs, you giant," she said. "I wish I attracted looks from women like her that you get more often than I get from the louts like those in the tavern."

He made a snorting sound then tossed his shirt over the glowgem to nightveil it so the room was suddenly enveloped in darkness.

"You are so oblivious," she said, "You could have had a night on the house with that girl, and not have to sleep alone tonight."

"How am I alone if you are over there accusing me of being oblivious to keep me awake all night."

"You are the same way back home. You are so preoccupied with your studies you never seem to notice the looks of the girls. You would be a catch for any girl or guy for that matter, except that you think too much."

He laughed. "You think too little, as befits your size."

"Watch it, monster, I will get you on the practice field again."

"I don't know that you will," he said, sadly.

There was long silence when the import of his words sunk in. "You didn't tell me you came through here," she apologized. "I'm sorry, it is just hard for me to realize."

"Nothing to be sorry about, Arinna. I knew this would be hard coming back, but like my Uncle once told me 'acknowledge the fear and embrace the change.' I had to come here, and I can't tell you how much it means to have you with me. If that Tarrow Cube reading is to be believed we are going forward into some troubled times."

"I don't know how I will keep out of trouble when I go back," she said quietly. "But it will be easier after I've seen where you will be; easier to picture you there."

"I know, but you'll manage," he said. "Your dad and Corvat and big Avril will try to keep up with you."

At the mention of the other second brand students who often spent time with the friends she laughed. "He is never sober enough to talk me out of trouble and she is never drunk enough to encourage me." Again there was silence. "But I will miss you."

"And I you, but not your chattering," he said with gentle humor. "At least not tonight. Go to sleep. We have to be up before first sun to get to the stable where I rented mounts."

"You were never specific; how much riding?"

"The ride to the hold will take two or three days. Four if we run into bad weather or you can't keep up."

"Four days? That long in the saddle?" She was a city girl and never comfortable on vornback.

He chuckled. "Only two if we ride very hard."

"Oh, great. I should have had more noodles at supper to pad my cute butt then, cause it's gonna hurt!"

✦✦✦

The sound of the door hinges squeaking was just enough to wake Erique. The room was still dark. Arinna was snoring across the room and there was no other sound in the late night house, which was why the slight noise seemed so loud.

Erique stayed perfectly still and worked to keep his breathing regular to mimic his sleeping-patterned breath. He opened his eyes the merest fraction to peer at the entrance as the door opened slowly to reveal two figures. They were backlit from the spilled light of the corridor outside. They appeared that both were male but it was clear they both were holding drawn daggers in their hands.

The shorter of the dark forms gestured toward the sleeping Arinna with his blade and the second, taller thinner one, moved almost soundlessly across the room toward the clerical student.

Erique watched the approaching stalker and the one moving toward his friend with increasing anxiety. He waited until the would-be assassin was almost at Arinna's bed then sprang from the pallet with the blanket in front of him to envelop his attacker.

At the same time Erique sent a single, powerful yell full of Priest-Voice at his friend. "Arinna, Danger!"

The effect was as if he had poked the redhead with a spear; Arinna was a warrior whose instincts for combat were almost always on the attack and so she erupted from the bed with her rapier already in hand and run the blade through the figure who was approaching her bed before he had a chance to parry.

At the same time Erique snatched his shirt off the glowgem to reveal that his friend had stabbed one of the sailors who she'd fought in the tavern.

The attacker Erique had enwrapped in his blanket fought his way free of the cloth but by then the clerical student hit the man with an open-handed blow to the neck. The blow struck the assassin with such precision that he was knocked out immediately and collapsed to the floor.

"What in Burkrum's Belt is going on?" Arinna cursed as she came fully awake with almost feral awareness.

She kicked the dagger away from where it had fallen by her attacker, who now was crumpled on the floor moaning and trying to hold back the flow of blood from the stomach wound where her sword had opened him up. He was screaming with terror as his life fluid gushed out between his fingers.

"What is going on in..." Gradax was at the door to the room with a cudgel in her hand and two of her security wardens behind her.

"These two snuck in with no good intent," Erique was already opening his healer's bag as he knelt beside the wounded man. He didn't waste time trying to negotiate with the madam. He took out a small vial and forced the moaning man to swallow the powder it contained. In a few moments the wounded man was unconscious.

When Erique looked up and saw the proprietress's expression he added, "It will slow the blood loss and hopefully save him. We don't really need to hear him whine when I stitch him up. If you would have one of your guards bring some hot water, I would be grateful."

He followed up his statement by bending down again to attend to the wounded man.

Arinna, after throwing on some clothes and tying up the other attacker, explained to Gradax who the two men were.

"I thought these two were a little funny," the Proprietress said. "They came in just after you did, only wanted one girl between them and then went into their room and were—well, quiet. They didn't even order drinks. But they paid for the whole night, so…"

"They must have followed us," Arinna said, "and waited till they thought we would be helpless in our sleep." She gave a feral smile. "Like we ever are, even then."

"I have to alert the city guard of this," Gradax said. "We are under civil mandate for our license." She started to send the remaining guard but Erique stopped her.

"Please don't do that; at least until I speak to you alone. For Etrar's sake."

She looked puzzled but sent the guard outside. Arinna made a noise and cleaned off her sword.

"Well?" Gradax asked. Erique explained why he had returned to Westral City and why he was headed into the highlands.

"And that is why if you call the city guards we will be delayed with needless questions, possibly for days." He sat back on his heels, his hands bloody. He began to clean his implements, having sewn up the wound on the fallen man, who still slept under the influence of the drug Erique had given him.

"The Shoutte of Shoutte?" she whispered. "I can see why. And why you had that worried look during Mozda's reading for your friend. It was too close to reality." She smiled and there was a tear in her eye. "Etrar was right about you, Erique. He would be very proud."

She pointed to the wounded man in front of the clerical student. "Will he live?"

"Yes," Erique said with a wry smile. "Arinna was still sleepy so she missed everything vital, though it will hurt him every time he laughs for quite a while."

"Then both of you head off," she directed. "I will hold them in here for a day or two. They will not dare tell anyone of this or they will have to admit they were taken by a sleeping girl and a priest."

"Thank you, Gradax," Erique said. "For me, for the clan and for Etrar. Thank you."

Arinna was already dressed and had gathered up her gear. "Better take a bath before you put on your kilt, big guy," she said to him. "I'll get your stuff together. I guess I'll be in the saddle sooner than we thought."

Then she smiled to the Proprietress, "I don't suppose the kitchen is still open? I've worked up a bit of an appetite frolicking with this tvekspawn."

CHAPTER SIX:
JOURNEY INTO THE PAST

As vorn were notoriously skittish beasts, Erique requested a very docile one specifically for his friend. The four-legged, antlered creature accepted an offering of fruit as a bribe from the redhead and let her pet its beak for some time before she even attempted to mount it.

"We'll take it slow until you two get to know each other." Erique said.

"I don't mean to hold you back," she said as she stroked the mane of the vorn.

"You will not," he said. "I haven't been on a vorn for a bit myself, you know. I could use to ease into riding. We will get to Stormrest when we get there even if we have to take more stops along the way. I really have allowed for this in my plans; we made good time with the portal travel—better than if we were two or three weeks sooner or later, the warp wizard said. That at least is good fortune."

"Thank you, Erique. I promise I'll get better with this anyway."

"Yes, you will," he smiled. "You get better with everything you put your hand to because you work at it."

She looked at him for a moment not sure how to take an actual compliment but just gave a shy grin in reply.

The two friends were able to be out of the city more than an hour ahead of the first sun's rise and off through the pass just as the beginning rays of the red sun pinked the land.

The terrain changed radically from the coastal plain of Westral City to broken foothills that lead into highlands. Arinna complained for the first half of the day but was too exhausted trying to stay in the saddle to keep up her complaints for the rest of the trip.

By the middle of the afternoon, they topped a small rise and came in sight of a stone ruin off to the side of the trail. There was a small pond nearby with a stream flowing into it that meandered under a section of the road that formed a stone bridge.

"Can we stop for some water for the vorn?" Arinna clearly wanted to have an excuse to dismount but would not give him the satisfaction of asking. It made him smile.

"It is best not to stay anywhere around these ruins," he replied. "There is a cool enough spring beyond over the next rise; we should push on to there."

"Why can't we stop here?"

"Notice that those stones and columns are in the Mephan style?"

She studied them in detail for the first time, grateful for the distraction from her discomfort. The ruins were a jumble of red and grey stone incised with crystal accents and images. All were clearly from some age ago.

"Yes. I can see some remains of Mephan script on some of those bigger blocks." She reined her vorn so she could stand in the stirrups to rest her posterior and look directly eye-to-eye with him.

"Why is there a Mephan Empire Style building here? I thought you said your people repelled their invasion."

"My grandfather did raise the clans to drive the empire out, but this is where they had established a main foothold—the furthest they were able to penetrate into the highlands in a permanent way. There are some other ruins off the side of the road, beyond those scrub brush and weeds."

"It does not look like a military base."

"It was not." He made the sign of the Kova. "This was a temple to the Mephan cult of the water goddess, a cruel and evil group."

"What Goddess? I've never heard of..."

"It is not a name spoken often as it is so vile." He lowered his tone to a whisper. "Ashun, the cursed is the name we know her as."

"Oh," she said. "My father once mentioned that name, but I did not know who it was."

"They gave human sacrifice to their goddess," Erique said. "And is another reason my people dislike outland religions. The Mephan Empire tried to force conversions in the highlands. And they did it with sword and noose, fire and dagger."

"This is as far as they made it?"

He smiled. "This is as far as they made it with an attempt at a permanent structure," he said. "The clans razed everything they built—any attempt at a fort or outpost in the highlands—almost the moment they built them. This was close enough to the coast that the clans were reluctant to venture here, but my grandfather eventually convinced them that the only way to keep the Empire out was to drive them all the way to the coast." He made the sign of the Kova again and a hand gesture she recognized as a ward of Zondra, the dual god/goddess of the highlands.

"This was the place of the final battle," he continued. "The slaughter was massive, in a fight that lasted for ten days with the Mephans bringing all their reinforcements from Westral City. They say even ancient shadowcraft was used against the clans but in the end, the Mephan invaders were crushed completely, the few survivors of the Mephan army fleeing to the city and taking ship, some say blowing into the sails themselves to move the ships faster to race home in defeat. It was the greatest moment in the history of the land."

He spoke with a pride in his homeland she had never heard before and it forestalled even a thought of a quip.

The two friends rode on with even the vorn quiet as if they too were aware of the ghosts of the place. The broken land among the scrub showed some chunks of worked stone and the thought in both of the riders was that the stones were grave monuments now to thousands of dead.

Even Arinna was quiet for a long time after they passed the ruins and when they first dismounted at the promised spring ten minutes further down the trail she had to work to find words.

"I don't care what you say," Arinna said, after they had led the vorn to the spring to drink and stood to make sure they did not over do it. "I know I am slowing you down. You should go ahead, just mark the trail."

"Don't be absurd, Arinna." He stepped off his own mount and stretched as she leaned into the spring to sip water herself. "I told you we will take whatever time it takes. We have to camp soon anyway, as it is too dangerous to travel at night."

"Yes but…"

"No," he cut her off. "I think we could do one more night under a roof. There used to be an inn not too far ahead of us; if it is still there you are safe for one more night from my cooking."

Her expression stayed dubious as they remounted and pressed on, all the more aware of how tired and saddle worn she was, so she welcomed the sight of the four buildings of the waystation a short time later. The first sun had set and the twilight was deepening.

"Greetings, Travelers." A young girl met the two friends as they rode into the low wall around the compound of the inn. She was dressed in homespun and barefoot, her long black hair a wild tangle and her wide smile showing a gap in her front teeth.

She turned back toward the main building and yelled, "Papa, Father, Wayfarers!! They look hungry!"

"She's perceptive, at least," Arinna joked as she slid off her vorn, grateful to be on solid ground again.

"Well, let's hope it is not too crowded," he said, "Sometimes at these inns, latecomers don't have much, they get only the leavings of the cookpot."

"But we left so early..."

"But someone may have left early yesterday and traveled slowly." He pointed out, "And people come from the interior, so they could be full up. Hope there are a few crumbs for you."

She moaned at the thought of no food and he laughed.

The two of them led their vorn to a corral that was off to one side. "That's funny," Erique said.

"What do you mean?"

"There are only three vorn in the shed by the corral," Erique pointed out. "At this time of the season there should be caravans—the first grow of nekot harvest is usually outbound already. And the station usually keeps extra vorns here to replace the pack animals that are worn out at this point."

The two friends began to unsaddle the beasts but before they had finished a broad-shouldered, thick-waisted, bearded man came out from the main building. He was unusual in that both beard and hair were so blond as to almost be white.

"Good day, travelers," the man greeted. "I am Reton. Please leave your mounts, our stable boy will tend to them—he's had little enough to do this turn. Please, head in relax. My husband is cooking up some fresh Avrum, greens and sweetbread for us all."

"I think I like your highland hospitality," Arinna smiled almost too glad to get away from the vorn.

"Is that a Cozen accent?" Reton asked.

"Yes," she replied with suspicion. She looked to Erique to see what her course of action should be.

"I haven't heard that since I landed in Westral City thirty years ago."

"I'm from Tolan, born and breed," she said.

"No, really?" he laughed hearty and loud. "I was born in the Bottoms but left to go to sea as a boy. But once I landed here, I met my husband and I became a landlubber!"

Erique and Arinna introduced themselves to the innkeeper just as a teenage boy came running out to attend to the vorn.

The innkeeper walked the two friends into the main building that had a large common room with a roaring fire in the hearth. There were half a dozen tables, but the only occupants in the room were the young girl they'd seen outside and a slim, dark, dark-haired man who was obviously related to the young girl from his look.

"Welcome, travelers!" the slim man said. "Sit, I will have food ready in a few minutes."

"Thank you, sir," Erique said.

"Girad," Reton said, "The dame is from Tolan!"

"No! Your hometown?"

"And the gentleman went to the Kovar Academy in the Bottoms."

"I grew up at the academy, actually," Arinna was a little surprised by the sudden popularity of her hometown. She accepted an ale from the dark-haired man and took a seat on a leather padded bench, sitting gingerly.

The two hosts sat with their guests, joined by the young girl—who indeed was Girad's daughter—and soon the five were a convivial group. Arinna and Reton were soon deep in reminiscences of The Bottoms.

"I haven't seen him so happy is a long time," Girad said to Erique after a filling meal that even sated the redhead's food craving. "Our wife died two years ago and with this season being so slack we have even considered moving back to the city."

"I am sorry for your loss," Erique offered. "You say it has not been a good season?"

"Yes," the jovial host said. "You two are the first guests in two moon turns."

"But what about the nikot caravans? There should have been the early crops by now."

"Not so, sir," Girad said. "Last year there were very few caravans and this year, none at all. And even the svor drives that usually bring us so many from all the clans have been sparse. Last was a small herd of Sween beasts almost three moon turns ago. None of the other clans have come through. It has been a tough season."

Erique pondered this news for the rest of the evening and when he and Arinna retired to their room he said, "I am afraid there is something very wrong in the highlands. Maybe many things."

"What do you mean?" She was delighted to have a soft bed to herself and a thick comforter, as she did not look forward to the rough days in the saddle or sleeping on the ground that were ahead.

"This should be the busy season for this inn, yet we are the first here in some time. And Girad said last year was bad as well."

"Could there be some sort of blight?"

"None of Cather's letters last year said anything about it. And a nekot blight would not cause the svor herds to be scarce—there are other foods that they can eat. Even wild grasses if all else is unavailable—they will each anything. From what he said, none of the clans have sent through shipments; that makes little sense since the clans fields are separated enough that even if there was a blight in one or two should not affect all the clans."

"So, your suspicions about how bad things are was right," she rose up on her elbow to look at him. "Something very bad has happened."

"Yes," he agreed. "But it is foolish to make guesses; we will just have to try not to be fooled by things on the surface. And be alert."

"Am I ever not?"

He laughed. "Only when you are distracted by hunger."

"Oh," she chuckled, "so you are saying all the time?"

"Good night, Arinna."

"Good night. Don't worry, Erique, you will find out what is going on and make it right."

"You have a great deal of faith in me."

"I'm here to back you up."

"Well, there it is then. Nite."

"Nite."

✦✦✦

In the morning the waystation family made a point of all being around for a hearty breakfast with their guests. The meal felt more like a family reunion with many jests and with Arinna showing the teenage boy and young girl some wrestling tricks (though she secretly showed the sister an escape or two from a hold she did not show her brother).

As the two friends prepared to leave, with a promise to their new friends that at least Arinna on her way back would spend time with Reton to talk about his and her adventures, Erique sang the family a song of friendship.

"*Sword of my soul, Edge of my heart, Blade of religion, Sharpe from the start, Sing of my hope, A song of tomorrow, Hymn of remembrance Love, pain and sorrow, cut through the shadows, Of death all to come 'Til victory sheathes you And my life's work is done.*"

Reton and Girad were both moved to tears and gave the clerical student a hug.

"Bless your quest," Reton said. "Bless your life."

+++

Arinna expressed no joy in remounting but felt refreshed enough to not complain, at least not constantly. They only stopped for a midday meal then continued until the Elder Brother, the larger and slower of the suns, was almost set and they stopped for an evening meal.

Shoutte said, "We had better make a cold camp; there are bandits in these hills as well as other clans who would love to take my head now that I am clearly marked by wearing the Shoutte kilt. So it is best to not advertise our presence any more than we have to."

Arinna looked up at him as she settled onto a log, resting on her stomach. "You told me lots of stories about all this land but didn't bother to tell me about how the 'other clans' were going to be hungry for your head."

"You didn't ask," he said with a wry smile. "With my brother dead there is not a clan leader and the other clan heads could see it as weakness; this is why it is necessary for the new clan leader to be installed quickly before anyone can take advantage with hostile action."

"Aren't you going to unsaddle those monsters?" she asked, when she saw he had only loosened the girth straps on the two, antlered vorns. The four-legged creatures were already feeding from a nearby bush, using their pointed beaks to snap off branches that they then stripped of the tasty berries. The fact that the hardy mounts would eat almost anything and thus could forage meant they did not have to bring very much feed for them.

"Better to have these beasts ready to ride, in case we have to move quickly."

This got her to lift her head and stare at him. "You are serious?"

"Yes." He turned to look at her. "I did not think much about it being this bad, I must admit, until I heard rumblings in the city of uneasy times among the clans. Though she had not heard about my brother's death, Gradax had heard that things were bad in the highlands. It seems to be worse than it has been in many years. Then with what we heard back at the way station I know she was not exaggerating. If there were no caravans outbound it means that the treasuries of the clans will be depleted and there could be hunger. And hungry people can become desperate. In truth the constant strife was one of the reasons I left; the constant chaos. It is a reason I have been troubled all day about letting you come on this trip…"

"Don't even try to send me back," she insisted. She had to work hard to look fierce from her position laying over the log and it made him smile.

"I knew you would say that, which is why I didn't speak up sooner. Tomorrow we will actually be in the land of the clans proper; then we have to be twice as alert."

"I still wish we could have just taken a warp portal directly to your home," she commented as she stood and massaged her behind.

"I told you, Arinna, warps and much of the crystal craft like the linguarings that work elsewhere would not function well once we left the coastal plain and not at all in the mountains. The closest any warp would come is the one outside of Westral City. It is why the clans are so closed off from so much of the Mephan and Cozen cultures. Even the Thorangians seldom venture across the frontier from the east to come into the highlands because of that. We are considered to be savages, a primitive land full of warrior beasts once one crosses the frontier. That very isolation has been, in many ways, our defense against outsiders."

"It is why you are so much of a barbarian?" she snickered. He gave her a cross look then sighed. When she saw he took her remark seriously she added, "I mean, I know one of the reasons you left was to see more of the world and all, as well as to study at the Academy."

He took some svor jerky from their saddlebags and handed some to her, sitting with his back to the log she had been draped over without speaking.

"I'm sorry," she said, "I didn't mean to…"

"No. You are right; Umbria is a primitive place compared to Tolan or even one of the smaller cities of the City States Confederacy. And with much less diversity than Thorangia. You saw yourself that Westral City was little more than a frontier settlement for all its attempt to be a real city it is little more than a way-stop to other kingdoms."

"All seaport cities are like that," she said. "And it seemed enough of a city to me. But I can see why you could feel it was little more than a place for people to load and unload on their way to somewhere else."

"Yes, I suppose it is not so bad as you say," he admitted, "but here in the mountains my people do not want outsider ways. Outsider food, religions, language, even war ways. Their isolation is something they embrace with fierce pride. And I am an outsider now."

She stepped around the log to rest a hand on her friend's broad shoulder. "I've seen it even in neighborhoods in Tolan," she said. "Each place seeks to think itself better, sometimes out of defense for the sure knowledge they are not. So much tribalism, even in cities, and I see how you might think they would see you as an outsider now, but you are from the Umbria, it is your home. And you bring only good ideas."

"I know," he patted her reassuring hand. "But I have been away so long and now I have come back to … to be their leader. And to be any kind of a leader I will have to convince them I am still Umbrian, still Shoutte and somehow win them to me. There are those who believe you can't change where you are from, who you are, but just as many who say the opposite. I have to lead my clan, so I must find a way for the both sides of that equation to accept me if I am to live up to the success my brother brought to them."

"But you said yourself that you believe in change, right? The Kova!" She reminded. "You have to believe you will be the agent for that positive change."

He attempted a smile. "I am not even sure what I want anymore. But you remind me that to serve the Kova I should be cheerful and ready for whatever comes. To the Rythem." He rose and hugged her. "You really are your father's daughter."

"And my mother's," she added. "That's where I get the cute from."

"I know," he agreed with a laugh. "From him you get the mean as well—at least on the training field. Let's get some rest. We will want to be up and away early."

Erique moved around the small clearing where they camped, arranging the underbrush in a wide carpet that circled the whole space. When he was satisfied with the result, he came back to set their bedrolls out by the log, where Arinna had dug a slight 'hip hole' in the soft earth underneath the improvised bed.

"Don't we need to stand guard?" Arinna asked. "I don't want to have you scare the future growth out of me again like at the contract house."

He shook his head. "That will never happen—I think you don't have any growth spurts left. Not to worry, the vorn are skittish enough to warn

...TO REST A HAND ON HER FRIEND'S BROAD SHOULDER...

us, I suspect." He settled down, only removing his boots and using the shoulder throw of his kilt as a blanket. He also set his straight sabre at hand beside him. "And you know I am a light sleeper; the real danger will not be until we get through the pass."

"As you say," she took off her boots and sword belt as well, also removing her svorskin shirt and leather jerkin so she was naked to the waist. She crawled under the blanket and snuggled into Erique's back, something they had done before when camping, having dubbed him a human stove for the warmth she leeched off him.

"Are you sure the vorn will be able to hear any intruders over my snoring?" she giggled.

"Good night, Arinna," he whispered. "Thank you for coming with me; this would have been much harder to do without you."

✦✦✦

Erique Shoutte was in the depth of a dream, seeing his father standing before him. He knew it was a dream because, though his father had been as he was before he died, the Kovar student was his own nineteen-year-old self.

"I will not have you spouting that Kova nonsense around here, boy," the elder Shoutte said. The two of them were in his father's keep room, the courtyard of Stormrest and the Shoutte lands spread out below.

"But Uncle Etrar said…"

"My brother is an idiot," the clan leader said. He was ramrod straight with a thick black beard, streaked with grey, and a long scar on his right cheek that flamed red when he was angry. It was violent red now.

"Zondra, the dual one, is our path, boy," The Shoutte said. "They have guided this clan for many years and no foreign gods or heathen ways will change that. They are all we need and all the clan will ever need."

"But … but Uncle Etrar healed m-mother when she was sick," the dream Erique said, with the stutter he had as a boy. He remembered saying the same words to his father, but when he was younger.

"Kova healer craft does not make up for his strange ways," The Shoutte said. The head of the clan stood and Erique found it odd that he was the same size as the father because he remembered the man towering over him. "You mind your war master and stay away from your uncle's heresy."

"But I want to learn the Kova!" Erique said, the stutter of his dream-self gone. "It is my hope and safety."

The Elder Shoutte raised his hand to strike the dream Erique and suddenly there was a snapping sound, and the clerical student was awake.

It was dark, so the moons had set. The night sky was dotted with stars, the air crisp and the nocturnal sounds strangely muted.

Erique was on his left side, Arinna's arm draped over his waist, his left hand touching his scabbarded sword. He stayed very still, listening hard. Beyond her breathing he heard some night birds gently singing and the sound of the breeze in the trees. And something else.

There was a cracking sound, very faint, off opposite the tethered vorns.

It could be a small animal, Erique thought, but his fingers moved slowly up the scabbard to the sword's handle. There was the soft crack of a branch and he knew with certainty that a first branch breaking had been what woke him.

The wind is flowing away from the vorn so they haven't gotten the scent of whoever is out there. He reached back with his right hand and gently prodded Arinna who moaned and slapped at his hand.

He closed his fingers on hers and squeezed hard. He felt her start awake.

"Sword," he whispered under his breath. Her body posture changed and she turned over so her back was to his and he could feel her shifting to reach for her own weapon.

Just as Erique's fingers wrapped around the grip of his sabre, the four attackers sprang from the darkness, splitting to pounce on the two friends.

The attackers fell on the two friends evenly, a man and a woman on Erique and two men attacking Arinna.

The petite redhead sprang up and threw her blanket ahead of her to tangle one of the swordsmen, then launched herself into a low thrust to send her rapier through the left leg of the second attacker.

Erique jumped to his feet with his sabre still in its scabbard, parrying a hacking cut at his left side from the male attacker. He whirled and snapped the sword toward the head of the second attacker that caused the scabbard to fly like a missile at the woman's face.

The woman instinctively batted the wood and metal scabbard away but this gave Erique the time to shoulder into her. The battle-scarred female tumbled backward over the log. This allowed the cleric to sprint to the center of the clearing before he turned to face the male intruder.

Arinna's first attacker freed himself from the blanket and slashed at the topless redhead. She accepted the attacks of the heavier sword with deflections from her rapier but had no room to maneuver. "Two!" she called out. "One wounded!"

"Two," Erique yelled back as both of his attackers were on him again. "Both hale and hearty!"

The man was shorter than the woman, and though broader had the same facial scars that were their clan marks. The hair of each of Erique's opponents was cut short and they wore boiled leather armor on their upper bodies and kilts.

Erique moved to keep the vorns at his back so the two attackers could not flank him. The ambushers' swords were wide straight blades, typical Highland weapons that were shorter than his saber. They were the typical of the mindset of the highland clans who preferred to work in close with their opponents, driving by ferocity and brutal strength more than any of the finesse that Arinna's father taught at the Academy.

That finesse in footwork and blade technique, combined with his long arms allowed Erique to keep the attackers at a distance and off balance, but he knew he could not do it for long.

CHAPTER SEVEN:
VISITORS WELCOMED

Arinna advanced to strike at her wounded intruder. This opened her left side and the uninjured man leapt in, slashing at her apparently unprotected flank.

The redhead's attack had been a feint at the fallen man, however, intending to draw the attack. As the uninjured man slashed at her left leg she spun to the right and drove the point of her rapier into the exposed armpit of the attacking man, penetrating just over the leather armor arm hole with carefully planned precision.

The stuck man screamed in pain, mortally wounded before he dropped in a spray of blood.

"Half of one," Arinna called as she withdrew her crimson-stained sword.

Erique's opponents were finding their rhythm as they pressed him back toward a stand of trees. The undergrowth and branches worked for him, however, with his longer blade since they could not swing unencumbered, but he could thrust unimpeded.

"Switch?" Erique called.

The two attackers had no idea what their victim meant until a red-haired wild tvek launched herself onto the back of the man, knocking him to the ground with the velocity of her sudden bodyweight.

As the female attacker took notice of the abrupt attack the Kovar clerical student took advantage of the momentary distraction to move on her. Erique made repeated thrusts and then lunged under a particularly sloppy slash of hers to drive his sabre's point into the bicep of the woman's sword arm.

Arinna meanwhile had clubbed her man into unconsciousness with her sword's pommel and stood over him in triumph.

All at once only the sounds of moaning wounded and the bleating of the vorns filled the night. Then Arinna giggled.

"Arinna!" Erique admonished as he stepped forward to tie the hands of the female attacker behind her.

The redhead gave him a smug look, cleaned off her rapier and re-sheathed it. She smiled and shrugged.

"Get my healer's bag," he insisted.

The petite girl continued to grin as she fetched his bag and he proceeded to clean and bind the wound of the woman. Arinna tied the hands of the man she had wounded in the leg, who, though it was not a terribly bad wound, was crying like a child

"Oh, shut up," she said as she secured him. She spoke in Cozen but when the man looked up at her without comprehension, she switched to the Umbrian that she had learned from Erique. "I said 'shut up' because unless you're crying for that one"—she pointed to the one she had killed—"you have no right to whimper. I've had worse wounds falling out of bed."

Erique finished binding the arm wound of the sullen woman attacker and came to work on the crying man's leg. Meanwhile Arinna secured the still unconscious man she had pummeled.

"Why did you attack us?" Erique asked the wounded man, also in Umbrian.

The man had stopped crying but was still whimpering. He was broad shouldered with a broken nose and a thick auburn beard. His watery blue eyes were full of tears. "Give me something for the pain, healer!"

"Why did you attack us?" Erique asked.

"Keep your mouth shut, Jundar," the woman snarled. Arinna kicked the woman in the flank, but the prisoner turned and spit at her. "Don't beg from this Shoutte or his bitch!"

Arinna kicked her again, harder, but restrained herself from punching the woman in the face. Instead she yelled to Erique. "They seem to know you!"

"They have clan scars from the Sween clan," he said. "But they would have had to be observing us in the daylight to know I was Clan Shoutte, since my kilt pattern would be hard to see in the dark." He had left the clan before his clan scars were earned, so though anyone who got a good look at him could tell he was an Umbrian Highlander, his clan would not have been so clear before he donned his kilt, which he did not do till they left Westral City.

"Give me some time with this beauty," Arinna said. She grabbed a hold of the scalp lock on the woman and pulled her head around to stare into the prisoner's eyes. "And I will have her singing truth chants out her arse!"

"No, Arinna," Erique said. "No highlander can be broken by threat or torture; least of all the Sween."

The female prisoner glared at him but nodded at the backhanded compliment.

"What do we do then?" Arinna returned the glare of the muscular woman and fingered her rapier handle hopefully. Erique frowned.

"Make sure they are tied securely and then get some rest; we have some very hard riding tomorrow and we will have to be all the more alert now."

Arinna started to object but realized it was useless so went to the wounded man and secured him and the unconscious man to trees—facing in opposite directions so they could not signal each other. She gagged them for good measure.

The Kovar student tied the woman to another tree and whispered, "Clanswoman, I came home to honor my brother. I do not look for contention or death, but I will not shrink from it. Tell whoever sent you when I release you that I am Shoutte and we do not retreat." He opened his shirt to show his skill brands. "And I am Kovar trained which should make all who would oppose me doubly fear my wrath."

The Sween woman said nothing, but even in the dim starlight it was clear that color drained from her face at the teen's statement.

+++

The two friends took turns keeping watch while the other slept undisturbed. The prisoners, hearty back-country stock, made no complaint but for an occasional moan of discomfort. The only disturbance was the sound of scavengers feasting on the corpse of the fallen attacker that

Erique had carried off some distance from the camp to leave in the brush, where the clerical student sang a transition song for the dead man.

Erique made the blessing sign of the Kova then of Zondra to honor the fallen clansman then sang softly, an old highland hymn for the man. *"My memories dim of a time of men, When truth and valor reigned, When just and friend were lived not penned, And love was a thing never feigned, Dual God on high when I die, Let them pyre me not on my wishes or hope, That fails, Let me ride out instead with a helm on my head, On a warship under full sails …"*

When he returned to the clearing the wounded woman looked at him strangely.

"You do him honor, Shoutte."

"He fought without cowardice, Sween," Erique said. "I could do no less."

She studied his expression to see if he was mocking her and when she realized he was not she said, "I am Konak, of the Sween. For my clansman Undar, I thank you."

Erique nodded, then went to sleep.

+++

All five combatants were awake as the Younger Brother, the smaller of the two suns, warmed the sky before the Elder Brother brought full light to the day.

Erique sang his morning truth chants softly while the prisoners looked on disapprovingly at the strange rites and then in awe as he did the first form of his martial exercises. The highlanders understood more clearly why they were bound and he alive when they saw his devotion to the warrior arts, spinning and striking with a ferocity and focus that was awesome to behold. He did both unarmed and sword forms, fighting phantom foes in the preset exercises that concentrated on nimbleness and skilled footwork. Though he performed them slowly they saw in them the seeds of his speed from the night before.

Arinna did her morning stretches and a hundred practice lunges then said a short pray to Yulin while Erique did his second forms. Afterward she enjoyed watching the stunned expressions on the prisoners as they watched while Erique did his last form.

The two friends were of different religions, yet both were tolerant in their dogma and ultimately were about trying to be better. And both were equally devoted to their separate ways.

When the two friends had packed up their gear they stood before the three stone-faced prisoners.

"You are going to kill us now," the woman said with finality. There was no fear in her voice and no anger just a resolution to what was to come, expecting the highland way.

Arinna looked at her then up to her tall friend, sighed and shook her head in disgust.

"As I said last night, we ride on, clanswoman," Erique said. "And we leave you as you are, Konak. You will be able to work your way free in time." He did not raise his voice, but his words were as sharp as his sword. "I promise you now, that if you cross paths with me or my friend again we will send you on your transition with no hesitation or regret. This is not weakness—it is mercy—the two are not the same. Take this to heart and tell it to all others who would oppose us."

The prisoners kept their own counsel and glared at the clerical student with a mixture of arrogance and surprise.

Erique gestured to Arinna and the two of them mounted their vorns and moved down the trail.

"I wish you had let me threaten them," she said when they were out of earshot of the prisoners. "With me at least they would know I meant it."

"I did mean it," he said casually.

"You can't fool me. You are soft hearted, everyone at the Academy knows that."

He shot her a dark look. "That was at the Academy, Arinna. Things here in the mountains don't allow for much discussion or equivocation. I showed mercy and here some—in fact, many— see that as weakness, but you know that is not so."

"I know," she admitted. "Father would be the first to say, 'be strong and you can afford to be merciful.'"

"Yes. And if I am to be The Shoutte I wish that to be known. Like those four, everyone needs to know if I do encounter any of them, I will strike first and question after if there are any to hear."

They rode in silence for a bit while she contemplated the import of his words, and the dark turn of his mood. "I have never seen this in you before, Erique."

"I have never been faced with so much responsibility, Arinna. Anything I do, if I am wrong, could cost many lives, hurt so many people."

"Don't think that way," she said. "You have handled everything that has come your way so far. You came alone to the Academy, overcame your stutter, your lung sickness and passed every test your have been faced with by the Masters. Besides, you have me to tell you when you do something dumb."

He laughed. "Well, that certainly takes the weight off my shoulders."

+++

They rode at a steady pace, faster than the day before but not so hard that they would tax the animals if they were suddenly called on for a burst of speed to escape ambush.

"I didn't think that that the cube reading was going to mean so much," she said after a time.

He looked over at her with a curious expression, "Well, what did you think it would mean?"

"I thought it was, just going to be, you now, fun. Just fun."

"It was based on a religious ceremony," he pointed out. "It was about summoning power—or at least asking the fates to whisper of that power—to the inquirer."

"But it's like the Yoni Stones. We used to play at asking questions all the time—is she cute—will he talk to me—will I pass the next quarter's tests—that sort of thing."

"Yes," he said, "but you said it yourself, '*you* were playing—and a yes/no /maybe questions are more a matter of chance than a request that calls the higher powers to answer."

"You're saying the stones are not real?"

"No. Belief gives many things power. I of all people believe that."

"But why did the Tarrow Cubes get so—so close. I can't believe that the girl Mozda was that skilled."

He laughed and when he saw that she was hurt was quick to add, "It is not the skill of the one who handed you the cubes, it is the caster; you! The Tarrow Cubes are tools that are more—precise than the Yoni Stones. A way of focusing energies from beyond the world we see to bring it into our world. Ask with intensity—as you did—and the results are more about you, what your self calls out to the powers. Your energy called to the forces of the universe—you spoke to the Rythem, if you will—and they answered."

She looked at him with a little awe. "You never talk about such things with me. I-I never realized how deeply you thought of such things."

"I am studying to be a priest, you know. We all study not just the Kova, but other religions as well. Your father was my instructor, actually in the comparative explorations. All knowledge of all religions benefits, even if it is not in line without out belief system."

"Like sword styles," she reframed the discussion in a comfortable world for herself. "One should know all you might encounter and, well, there is always something with each style that you can learn from."

"Exactly," he laughed, "see, you're a philosopher and theologian and didn't realize it!"

If she could have reached across the space between their mounts she would have hit him, instead she made a farting noise and they both laughed.

+++

After a time as their mounts picked their way around a rockfall on a narrow, rough section of the trail Arinna's vorn jostled her when its foot slipped before it recovered which startled her to squeak a curse.

"My blistered butt has been destroyed by this vorn," she complained, as she dismounted to allow the vorns to rest for a few minutes, "and now my back from sleeping on the ground. If I don't earn a sainthood for making this trip, I don't know what would qualify me!"

Erique snickered and threw her a piece of svor jerky. "I'll put in a word with the Council of the Elders at the Academy, but they will have to examine your butt to be sure the blisters are real and not manufactured for attention."

She chewed the jerky, turned, and dropped her breeches to flash him her bottom. "I'll give them a full show to get a shrine to me."

He laughed. "You'll blind them with that whiteness!"

"The shrine of the holy white cheeks," she giggled, as she redressed. "I think I'll start composing truth chants to my derrière while we ride today."

"I shall be your first acolyte," he joked, while he tightened the girths of their mounts. "But we had best be on our way, your Holy Buttness; if we hurry we can make the village below Stormrest by dark."

"Holy Buttness," she chuckled, as she settled the new talisman of worship gingerly onto her saddle. "That's me!"

CHAPTER EIGHT:
IN THE LAIR

The country became increasingly rugged and rocky as the two friends rode deeper into the foothills and then through a pass. Arinna remarked about how the air pressure had changed.

"We are fully through the pass and we have been rising steadily, though gradually for hours now," Erique said. "Also, technically we have been on Clan Shoutte lands for the past two hours."

"This doesn't feel like a mountain top."

"True, but this is well above sea level and the plain beyond these broken hills extend across most of the highlands," he said, "a broad, flat plateau in reality, surrounded by some more rugged hills, some true mountains. It is called 'The Shield of the Clans.' There are only a few passes through."

The two suns burned bright in an all but cloudless sky and there were just a few kukora birds, their leathery wings the only sound as they swooped low to investigate the ground for the flightless, burrowing avrum they favored as prey.

The two friends passed through areas of broken low hillocks and thick brush along the rough track—more spots that could provide attackers the cover from which to ambush travelers.

"My hackles are on fire," the redhead said, in a cold whisper, as they rode through a last narrow defile to come fully out onto the rolling highland plain.

"I know," Erique reined up and dismounted near a copse of trees. "So, it is best we announce ourselves properly from this point on." He cut a long branch, stripped it of leaves and then produced a flag from his saddlebags that had the red and black-feathered dragon symbol of Clan Shoutte embroidered on it.

"This is fully my clan's domain now," he said, remounting. He seated the butt of this improvised flag on his stirruped right foot. "This should keep us safe from attack, at least from my own kin."

"Should," Arinna looked around. "But from what you keep saying, maybe not even from your own people. You do not inspire me to relax, so

I'll keep my blade loose in the scabbard if you don't mind."

There were no problems, however, and before long they were moving through herds of blue-green svor on either side of the trail. The herds of slow-moving lizards, which provided the primary meat for the highlanders, were watched by several young herders on foot who moved among them.

Those same herders, all tall, dark-haired highlanders like Erique, observed the two with suspicion as they rode by but made no move to contact them.

"Not a very friendly bunch," Arinna glanced at the herders who glared back at the friends as if in challenge. She noted that even the herders had short, broad highland swords on their hips. "Or have they never seen a redhead?"

"Not one your size," Erique said with an unmanly giggle. "Or one so cute."

Her stare in response did not have the intended effect of striking him dead so she hissed under her breath—but loud enough for him to hear. "You have to sleep some time, giant!"

They both laughed.

For an hour they moved past the herds and then the road wound between cultivated fields of nekot plants that stretched to the horizon. The tall stalks provided feed for the svor and the fibers of the leaves were woven into the cloth for clothes, particularly the kilts of the mountainous region.

"It is the crop that keeps the highlands solvent, along with the svor meat which we export," Erique explained. "The clan convoys bales of nekot each spring to the seaport for export. Not much else survives the winter frosts, though there are some hearty varieties of tubers that provide much for bread and such. At least that is how the economy worked before," He said with a dark shadow across his remembrances.

Arinna took it all in, making eye contact with any of the clan herders and returning their glares with her own challenge. Her mood was not improved by her discomfort in the saddle and she was torn between asking Erique to stop and let her rest, and gritting her teeth to push on so the journey would end sooner.

In a small dip in the landscape they spotted a figure racing through the heavy underbrush with the sound of click-barks of a tvek pack in pursuit. The four foot lizards were snarling and obviously hunting the figure for a meal.

"There," Arinna called, "That man needs help…" Then she stopped as the figure became clear for just a moment as it lopped with an odd gait between two clumps of bushes.

"Not a man," he said and she realized he was right. The exposed figure was man-like it was sure, but like a crude image of a man, a furred, hoofed thing. It had a face with two eyes and short snout with small tusks.

"It's a goranga," Erique said. "They usually don't come down into the valleys."

As the two friend watched the furred animal turned to face the four legged killers and a savage battle ensued with the six pursuers. Arinna's instinct was to move to help the lone figure, even if it was not human, but before she could react on it the complexion of the fight changed.

The faux man-beast smashed the first of the tveks with a crudely shaped fist and grabbed a second by the throat where it sank in its fangs.

Just then two mounted warriors in Shoutte kilts raced up and before the goranga could kill any more tveks—obviously their hunting pack—used long weighted poles to smash into the head of the beast.

It dropped unconscious and the riders had to beat back the tveks to keep them from savaging it.

"A party from the stronghold," Erique said. "The skin of that beast is valued, but they would not have risked chasing it down into the valley so I can only assume it came down on its own to hunt from the clan herds."

The riders threw the carcass of the goranga over the haunches of a vorn and allowed the tveks to feed on their fallen comrades.

"Very brutal," she said as the reptiles tore at the flesh of their own kind.

"It is the highland way," he said in a flat voice. "This is what I have come home to."

+++

After another hour they topped a rise and found themselves in view of the clan fortress of Stormrest with its village spread out before the hold. All were on the edge of Lake Shoutte, a vast body of water that stretched to the horizon, beyond which were snow-capped peaks.

The hamlet of Stormrest was not much of a town, merely a collection of some two-dozen huts. It was really just for clan retainers who worked the fields and nearby herds and who would flee to the hold in time of danger. They were not real dwellings like a homestead would be, but simply consisted of small stone and mud huts and as many outbuildings and lean-tos.

The simple structures spread out on either side of the muddy road. At the lane's end the drawbridge spanned a deep channel that ran out of the

...IN VIEW OF THE CLAN FORTRESS STORMREST...

lake. When the bridge was up, the channel acted like a swift-moving moat, effectively cutting the stronghold off into its own ad-hoc island as it was built on a spit of rock to rise above the lake waters.

Beyond the bridge on the promontory of rock, Stormrest, the seat of Clan Shoutte perched like a predator ready to pounce, occupying the whole spit of land with sheer cliffs all around and seeming to arch over the lake. The stronghold was hewn from the same red rock on which it sat and in the twilight of the single sun it looked as if it was painted with blood. And in many ways, with the history of clan conflicts, it had been.

Erique halted his mount at the edge of the village and just sat quietly staring ahead.

"Are you alright?" Arinna asked in a hoarse whisper.

The dark-haired clerical student took a deep breath, inhaling the familiar scents. *All the same and yet so different*, he thought. *So many memories and so few that really are good ones. Did I really have to come back? Is it the right decision?*

"Erique?"

"I'm fine," he said hesitantly after a moment, though it clearly was not true. "But I really never gave any thought to coming back before; not really. It is hard to take in now that we are really here, and why I have come back. Everything within me is in conflict."

Guards could be seen on the battlements of the stronghold, though the portcullis was up and the gate was open and the bridge-door stretched across the channel.

"Those are traders coming out," Erique said, as they watched a dozen or so carts leaving the fortress. "They will close the gates at nightfall and raise the drawbridge. Even in times of peace the hold is sealed at night. With what I have heard of the unease in the highlands I am not surprised to see the battlements manned so fully. There really is no long-term peace here in the highlands."

Arinna continued to stare at the building, transfixed by the sight of the hold. "It looks like a great beast crouched ready to spring. How many are in there?"

"Normally in the regular complement at all times is about two hundred in the hold, but these villagers and the farmsteads nearby will come into the hold as well if hostilities become bad. We are here at svor roundup season, so many will be off, I expect, attending to the herds; even with my brother's death the work of survival must go on as usual. Cycles and traditions are strong here."

"We are attracting a lot of attention just standing here," Arinna said, shifting uncomfortably in the saddle and leaning forward to take pressure off her backside. And out of habit she checked her rapier to see it was comfortably loose in its scabbard.

The villagers, who probably did not see many strangers to begin with, were starting to gather in doorways at the sight of the mismatched pair.

Two little children in ragged kilts walked up to stand directly beside Arinna and looked up at her. When the redhead looked down at them and made a face they both giggled and raced away.

"You haven't lost your power to frighten," Erique said attempting to distract himself. "That is a constant, at least."

"Could that be you, Erique?"

A voice from one of the huts drew the attention of the two new arrivals.

The dark-haired young woman who stepped out of the hut entrance, arms full of scrolls, had her cheek tattooed with the clan mark of Shoutte. She was about Arinna's age, but like many highlanders, considerably taller.

"Cather?" Erique jumped from his mount as his sister dropped the scrolls and ran toward him.

Arinna dismounted and tied off their mounts to a hitching post while the two siblings embraced in a long hug.

The two ragged little children ran back around the hut to which they had retreated with a third, younger child, her face smudged with dirt. The trio gathered in a circle around the redhead. They stayed just out of reach but stared up at her with awe.

Arinna grinned and offered some Svor jerky to the leader of the little group, holding out her hand with a wide smile. The little leader hesitated for a moment then darted in and took it with a giggle before she then tore it into three pieces to distribute among the others showing true clan spirit.

After a long moment, the two siblings stepped away to arm's length and regarded each other with wide smiles.

"You are fully a woman now, Cather." He spoke with wonder in his voice, reconciling the image of her from when last he saw her and now.

"And you are fully a man, big brother!" Cather looked past him to Arinna and when she spoke the three children ran off again. "Who is your little friend?"

Arinna bristled at the description and Erique laughed.

"Oh, sister," he said, "she is not so little as she looks, though she is cute, eh?"

Arinna made a little growling noise but before she could launch herself at Erique, the dark-haired girl, who was only an inch or so shorter than her brother, gave a shy smile.

"Yes, she is cute," the Shoutte girl said. She extended her hand. "Hello, I am Cather, Erique's sister."

Arinna was so disarmed by the gesture and the much taller girl's attitude that she extended her hand and took Cather's. The two women held the handshake for a long moment, their eyes locked.

"I ... um, I'm Arinna Cabal," the redhead finally said, blushing. "I'm Erique's friend. Just his friend."

"Just his friend?" Cather's smile widening. "That is good to know."

Arinna's blush deepened.

Erique had a hard time suppressing a chuckle. "Starting already, Arinna? I'll have to write your father." Once more her death stare at him had absolutely no effect.

"We had better get up to the hold," Cather finally said, turning from Arinna to look at her brother, "They close the gate for the night soon even if I'm out here. And word will have to go out to the homesteads that you have returned before the night comes."

Cather called to the children who had popped around the hut again and had them join the three in gathering up the scrolls the girl had dropped. Arinna gave each of them another small piece of jerky from her saddlebags as reward and they gleefully sucked on them as they ran away. The three adults walked the vorns through the village.

"I was afraid you would not come back, brother." She almost whispered her statement, her features tight with worry.

"How could I not?"

She looked at him with knitted brows. "Who knows what your strange religion calls for," she said, very seriously. Erique recoiled as if from a blow.

"Hey, it is not a strange religion," Arinna said, before Erique could speak. "It is a good religion."

"Are you one of those Kovar as well?" Cather said with a sharp tone in her voice. They were walking over the drawbridge now and from the activity at the hold's entrance it was clear Erique had been spotted and they knew who he was.

"No," Arinna snapped back, "but I would be proud to be. My father is."

"What are you then?"

"More than you can handle," Arinna shot back. "And I worship the Goddess Yulin."

"Really?" Cather arched an eyebrow. "More?"

The two of them exchanged a look as the three stopped at the entrance to the hold.

"The Shoutte has returned!" Cather called up to the guards on the walls.

The guards picked up the cry that then was taken up from within the fortification and echoed. "The Shoutte has returned." It was soon repeated many times with each iteration sounding more excited.

Arinna and Cather kept eyes locked and it was clear each was ready to throw a sharp remark at the other and was just waiting for new provocation.

"You can stop dueling now," Erique said to the two women. "I think there will be enough battles ahead for all of us without you two brawling."

The trio entered the wide courtyard of the stronghold where the everyday activity of the fortress had come to a halt as the news spread of Erique's arrival.

Across the open courtyard space, around the perimeter of the yard and up against the curtain wall were several stone buildings that housed a blacksmith shop, a harness and leather worker's stall. There was also a stone, circular granary, a stable and a central well.

Beside these was a clearly marked practice area with pells and weapon racks where young warriors were in the midst of a training session. They stopped, practice weapons in hands and turned toward the gate when the new arrivals entered the yard.

It seemed that most of the stronghold residents flocked to the windows and galleries to catch a glimpse of the returning clan leader who had left them as a stuttering, skinny boy and returned as a broad-shouldered man.

Arinna looked up nervously at the battlements where curious guards had turned from the outer wall to look down at the new arrivals. The redhead had to work hard not to stare back at them in challenge.

"Just like with those little ones, I feel like I am on display," she whispered.

"You are." He smiled. "And so am I."

The murmur of voices rose to chorus levels till the three stopped in the center of the yard and Cather called out, "Behold, Erique of Shoutte has returned. My brother has come home!"

"You're a big deal," Arinna observed. "They seem happy so see you."

"For the moment," the Kovar clerical student said with a wry grin. "I suspect that will change soon enough."

Servants swarmed up to the group and relieved them of their mounts and the scrolls, lingering to get a closer look at the arriving pair and sheepishly trying not to stare before they took the mounts to the stables. It caused Arinna to giggle.

"I really do feel like a captured exhibit. I hope they don't put us in a cage."

"It won't be hard to find one big enough for you, at least."

She stuck her tongue out at him so he added, "If they do you can hope they start throwing treats at us."

"Come to think of it, I am hungry," she said. "We made it in time for dinner, right?"

"My lord." An older warrior that Erique remembered from long ago stepped up to face Erique.

The elder Shoutte was half a head shorter than the lithe clerical student and thick with age, but not with fat and was still formidable looking. Their family resemblance was clear. "I am in pain for the reason, but rejoice in your return, Erique."

"Thank you, good uncle Kurvan," Erique greeted. "It is good to see you and the hold so well; I know your stewardship under my brother is surely one reason for its prosperity."

The older man bowed his head in acknowledgement of the compliment. "The Shoutte's suite of rooms await you." He gestured to an older woman in simple clothes who stood nearby awaiting orders. "Davorna here will bring you and your servant to the suite."

"Servant?" Arinna whispered with a bit of a hiss.

"This is my friend and equal, Dame Arinna Cabal of Tolan, Kurvan," Erique corrected before the redhead could react fully. "She will require a room of her own. Near mine, if you would so kind, Davorna."

"Of course, lord," the steward nodded without acknowledging his *faux pas*. "There is a room down the hall from your suite, as you know, that can be opened for her."

"That will be most acceptable, Uncle."

The servant, Davorna gestured into a doorway that led into the heart of the hold. Arinna grabbed her personal saddlebags while Erique held onto his healer's bag.

"I will see you at dinner, brother," his sister said with a wide smile.

"We have much to discuss," he kissed her on the forehead like he had as a child. "We have so much to talk of."

"Yes," she agreed. "But I suspect dinner will not be the best place to speak about some of those deeper things." He caught her tone and nodded, sure there was some dark undertone to her request.

There is indeed something amiss here he thought. *I suspect I have come into more strife than I could have guessed.*

CHAPTER NINE:
DECISIONS

The clerical student and the red-haired swordswoman followed the older servant through the stone hallways of the stronghold and up stairs to the top floor of the tower keep. The stonewalls were old and polished, made of the same red-tinged stone as the rock on which the hold was built. All the walls were hung with tapestries telling the history of the clan.

There were both glowgems and older torch sconces along the walls, attesting to the age of the building—from a time before crystal glowgems had come to the highlands.

"This was my father's and then my brother's quarters," Erique pointed as they reached the top landing. It opened onto a short corridor with several doors, all opened at the moment. "As they were my grandfather's before them. From here the destiny of Clan Shoutte and indeed of the whole the highlands was decided and controlled. It feels strange to be here, like this and to think it will become mine if I am chosen."

"Your … friend may use these quarters, lord," the servant said quietly, indicating an open door on the left.

"Thank you, Davorna," Erique said. "I know the way to The Shoutte's rooms."

"All is in readiness," she said. "I will have, bread, fresh fruit and cool wine brought up and have the linens changed in the guest quarters."

"Oh good," Arinna said. "Food!"

"And hot water to wash," the new lord-to-be asked. "I think we need that as well; I have returned to the highlands and the highlands seem to have decided to return to me as well."

"Most certainly. I took the liberty when I heard of your arrival to begin the process. A bath is being heated now." She bowed and turned to go but he stopped her with a hand on her shoulder.

"Tell me, clanswoman, Davorna. What are the people's feelings on this— my brother's death and my return?"

She looked at him from beneath hooded eyes, a sidelong glance to Arinna. She pursed her lips in distaste. It was clear she considered the outsider a danger.

"She is my confidant," he said nodding to Arinna. "Anything you could say to me you could say to her. And I promise you may speak freely. I will take no offense. I seek only knowledge, not reason for remonstration. I have been away a long time and would know the mind and heart of our people."

She blew air out of her lips and shook her head. "There was darkness in Lord Atrum's death. None will speak of it openly, but—Zondra help us—I fear shadowcraft. Wizard work such as the cursed Mephans brought to the land." She hissed the words as if the mention of the island nation was a curse in itself.

She paused for a moment then added, "And, begging your pardon, but indeed you have been gone a long time—out-country ways are not well thought of among the clan."

"But you do not know what they are."

"And do not want to know, m'lord. Zondra is all we folk need; the dual-faced one provides." She set her jaw and it was clear there was nothing more to be said.

"Thank you for being honest, Davorna," Erique worked to keep his expression open and a smile on his face. "You may go, kinswoman, your service appreciated. May you stay in Zondra's light."

"M'lord," she curtseyed and quickly left.

"Well, you weren't exaggerating about how they feel about outsiders here," Arinna said.

"The highlands resist change, Arinna," he stared at the landing where Davorna had gone and shook his head. "And I have sworn my life to that very principle. Zondra has guided the clan forever; they were never open to outsider ways and then in my grandfather's time they came to fear all outsiders since the Mephan invasion. I am as much an outsider now as one of those invaders."

"Stop it, Erique. Is this worship of Zondra so very different?"

"Tradition is everything here. Anything new is suspect. Even if it helps the people; it was difficult for my father to press the nekot export treaties even though it was clear such an action would help the clans at appoint of harsh winters that were reducing feed for the svor herds. Only his force of personality made it happen and then the people accepted it for the prosperity it brought, even while still disliking the very thought of change. Like angry children who hate the idea they like the food their parents make them eat and rebel just out of spite."

"So you just have to convince them you are amazing."

"Is that all?" He laughed and shook his head. "Why didn't I think of that?"

She threw her saddlebags on the bed in the room that had been pointed out for her—a corner room with one small, high window and a small fireplace—then walked with her friend to his rooms down the hall.

The Shoutte of Shoutte had a suite of rooms that took up the whole back half of the floor in the tower. It consisted of a large entry chamber and an office with windows that furnished a wide view of the village and plain below; beyond that was a small anteroom and then a bedroom with a large fireplace and built in stone and crystal tub.

"This outer room alone is bigger than father's whole suite at the Academy Kova," Arinna said as she peeked over the sill of the window at the courtyard below. "But with these windows, it must be hard to keep warm in the winter."

Erique smiled. "They put crystal shutters up." He walked to the desk and ran a hand over the worn, carved Ovar wood of its surface, then stepped to the window. "From here The Shoutte can see to the horizon where the Shoutte lands butt into the Clan Kreill, beyond the lake in that direction. Two day's ride the other way is Sween lands." His tone was dark.

Arinna noticed his tone and looked back at him. "Are you sure you are alright?"

"Yes. It just seems so strange to think that desk is mine now; I remember standing at it and it seemed … so much bigger when last I saw it. I used to come to look out this window and my father would tell me that our land was the clansfolk who lived on it and that he was their servant and must always be strong for them. I did not understand it quite then, and I just don't know if I can be strong that way now that I do understand."

Arinna walked over to him and put a hand on his arm. "How can I help, Erique?" When he looked at her questioningly, she added, "I mean, how do you want me to act? I know I can be … uh…"

"A pain?"

"Confrontational," she completed with a virtuous pose. "And I know my differentness is a problem. I can leave if it will make it easier for you."

He grinned. "Thank you, Arinna, but while they have very seldom seen a red-haired person and I am sure never seen anyone like you, it is me that is the problem. I am the one who is tainted by the outside world."

"It makes no sense," she mused. "To turn away from things just because…"

"No," he said, "You were raised in Tolan, a city where many cultures and even many religions are tolerated. In fact, all of Cozen is a tolerant country as well, which is why the Academy was founded there. Yet you know that things that were different made people insecure and the Kovar are not popular in some quarters even there. Umbria respects only strength; to endure to overcome and to that end they place their faith in the God/Goddess of two aspects, Zondra and the traditions of the old days, real or imagined."

"Yes, but if I am…"

"Be at ease, all will be By the Rythem. I would not have you be anything other than who you are, to behave any other way than you do. Your friendship, since my first days at the Academy, is part of my strength, Arinna. It always has been. Along with my belief in the Kova, it has sustained me in even the darkest times."

She worked to keep from showing too much emotion. "I'm going to go to my pitiful little room," she turned quickly away. "If there is any warm water left over after you wash your massive body, send some over my way."

✦✦✦

The feast hall of Stormrest was not full when Arinna and Erique entered it; there had not been enough time for the word to go out to the outlying Shoutte clansfolk before the meal and many of the hold's forces were out for the svor roundup, but there were still over a hundred at the long tables spread throughout the room.

The room had a vaulted, two-story ceiling, wide doors at each end and galleries along two sides where musicians played flute and drums while the clan members ate. It was central to the hold and had two large fireplaces to warm the room in the dead of winter, though they only had low fires going at the moment.

Erique had coached Arinna on the etiquette before they entered the hall. Though not so different from Cozen customs at first, the small details—the passing of food or drink only to the left or the need to spill the first drop of each cup in honor of Zondra (into a bowl provided)—were very important customs to observe. That and many other small Highland traditions were overwhelming to the redhead who tended to attack food as she did any live opponent.

"I don't know about all this, Erique," Arinna admitted. He had tried to prepare her in their rooms for the feast after both had dressed in their best clothing by sitting down to a mock meal but it had been a frustrating experience for her. "It seems like there are so many little things. I feel like a rank beginner student at the Academy."

"You will be forgiven any but the most egregious mistakes, Arinna. You are a true outsider. It is I who will be judged in exacting detail. I am the one who must prove I am a highlander and a Shoutte to my core, that I have not been contaminated beyond repair. And I am not sure myself how much I am a highlander anymore. Even my accent is tainted by speaking Cozen for so long."

"Hey," she had said with a grin that was an attempt at humor. "That's the best accent in the world."

When they entered the hall the two friends were seated at a raised dais at one end of the room facing the long tables of the rest of the clan. Arinna was seated at Erique's right where a Lord's mate would normally be and Cather sat to his left.

"Atrum did not marry and had no issue from any partner, though there had been discussions with other clans in hopes of forming alliances," Erique said when he explained the seating arrangements.

"So, will they push you into a marriage that was intended for him?" Arinna asked. After observing every custom she could as she attacked her second helping of svor steak as if it might be snatched from her at any moment. She had remembered to let a drop spill from each cupful but it was the only one of the customs she had remembered to observe in full.

"No," the heir to the clan leadership said, as he ate slowly. He made sure to tap his knife to the table before each bite, as was the custom to dispel evil influences and taint from the meat. Even he had trouble recalling all the little rituals that were the traditions of the clan—some so obscure no one could remember their origins. "I doubt any other clan will align with someone as different from themselves as I have become. I am not highlander enough for many."

Erique saw so many familiar faces that were at the edge of his memory yet looked back at him with suspicion, not the devoted or caring faces of his past. For a long moment he wondered why he had truly come back. Was it to confront them all and say, *'I have prospered despite you?'* Was it hubris, or duty?

"There is truth in what you say, brother," Cather said. "If you can not gain the trust of the Shoutte you have no hope of any allies in the highlands at all."

"Well spoken, m'lady," Kurvan said. He sat beyond Arinna and spoke over her head to the raised chair where Erique sat. "I am afraid she has hit upon a relevant point that must be considered in any plans going forward."

"I am more than well aware of that, uncle," Erique said. "And hope our people will come to know me, respect me and know that I am still one of them."

"But are you?" A voice from beyond Cather spoke up. It was from a bulky, bearded Shoutte clansman named Brendar. "You have given yourself to another religion and have turned your back on the true dual God by leaving for foreign lands and adopting foreign ways."

Erique took a deep breath and exchanged a look with Arinna. She raised an eyebrow and inched her hand toward the meat knife on the table but he shook his head. The clerical student turned to face the cousin who had spoken and let his expression stay neutral.

"I hear you, kin Brendar," Erique said quietly and sincerely meant, "And I understand how you feel."

He swallowed hard. He'd known the moment would come when he had to speak before the clan and had dreaded it. He had dreamt of it all the way down from Tolan and yet had never been able to hear the words he would speak in that dream/nightmare that was too be.

Now the moment had arrived. When last most of them saw him or heard him, he was a skinny, sickly child who had to fight to push words out of his mouth to be understood. His stutter had been a wall between him and others. Now the years of training in Priest-Voice and all his time at the Academy Kova were to be put to the test. He recalled Etrar's words, *'Always be brave—never lose the fear, but never let it stop you embracing change'* and knew what he had to do to gain the respect that would allow him to rule.

He said a prayer "by the Rythem," to himself, took a deep breath and stood. Every eye in the room turned toward him and voices began to babble.

He held up his hands in a gesture that called all to a heavy silence. Then he raised his voice so all could hear him, putting just a touch of Priest-Voice into it in hopes to draw them in sympathy to his words. He spoke to all but looked directly at the burly relative who had spoken.

"I hear your voice, Cousin Brendar," Erique began. "I hear all your voices clearly, Clanskin. I know you do not trust lowland ways, but know that I am Shoutte. All Shoutte. I was born Shoutte and no amount of time away can change that. I would not have come back if it were not so, to the land and home that is in my blood, my heart and my soul."

There was a murmur among the tables but no one spoke out.

"This is my home; our home, but it is not the whole world. You cannot keep the world or its ways out of the hold any more than you can keep the wind from a distant shore from crossing our land. If you do not understand the ways from outside they can and will hurt you. You all know that to know a prey or an enemy to protect yourself and if you want to prevail over a prey you should know their ways and habits. I hope you will realize that no one knows those low country ways like I do, but to understand them is to know what to avoid in them as well."

"We don't need your godless ways," Brendar said.

"Not godless," Erique retorted. "I have embraced the Kova but I have not turned my back on Zondra; that is not what the Kova is. It accepts all."

"Blasphemy," a cry came from the back of the room. Then a second and a third voice took it up and the murmurs became a chorus.

"Turning away from the Dual One is what lead to The Shoutte's death!"

"A curse!" another one cried. "Someone called up a shadowcraft curse."

"Hold!" Kurvan yelled. "This is the elect you accuse."

Arinna looked to her friend and he saw she had the meat knife in her lap, ready for use.

"I stand before," Erique said suddenly in a loud voice that had the tone of a proclamation. "I stand before!"

There was a sudden dead silence in the hall followed by a gasp from the table and Cather shot to her feet.

"Brother, no!"

The hall erupted into cries of "yes!" and "not now! 'it is too soon!"

Arinna asked, "What are you talking about?"

"I have to do this, Cather," Erique told his sister. To Arinna he said, quietly, "This is the only way, Arinna, please be patient and stand by me in this. All will be clear soon."

Kurvan stood and faced Erique. "Erique, you can not invoke at this time; it is disrespectful to your brother."

"It can not wait," Erique said in a shape whisper. "Discord in the clan is dangerous, you know that. If these rumblings are not stopped, that would be more disrespect to Atrum. I must stand as soon as possible so that all will know there is unity in Clan Shoutte. And that I am Shoutte."

"What is going on?" Arinna stepped to beside her friend. "Somebody tell me!"

"Leave him, girl," Cather moved next to the redhead. "He has invoked a right that can not be stopped once called down."

"Do you understand, boy, what you are doing?" Kurvan asked the clerical student. "You have just returned, you have no alliances, no backing. You are not experienced…"

"I do understand and I say again, 'I stand before.'" Erique looked to Brendar. "Do you call me to stand, Brendar of the S-Shoutte?" Erique felt a bubble of fear within him, about to burst. He almost lost control of himself and had to force himself to take calming breaths to maintain his outer composure and prevent the stutter he had not had for years from returning. He fought to keep it controlled and summoned Kovar breathing techniques.

The bearded cousin surveyed all around him as the people in the room looked from each of the two men to the other.

"I do, Erique of the Shoutte." The bearded man rose and stood at arm's length from his cousin. "Before this assembly and the true Dual God Zondra, I call you to stand."

The hall went suddenly quiet, as if before a storm.

"Zondra comforts the strong and gives strength to the weak." All the voices in the hall intoned the prayer at once, save Arinna who stared at her tall friend as if he had sprouted wings. Even Erique said the prayer, but added, "To the Rythem" softly under his breath.

CHAPTER TEN:
PREPARATIONS

"Are you insane, Erique?" Arinna was furious, waving her arms and pacing back and forth in the anteroom to the great hall.

"I have to do this, Arinna. I told you when we encountered those Sween attackers that the clans respect only strength and as long as they think my being Kovar makes me weak they will never listen to me; I can never guide them if they have no faith in me." The two friends were alone in the small space, the clerical student having designated her a 'shield aid' to his cousin's challenge to combat.

"But this 'stand' thing…"

"It is an old ritual putting our fate in the hand of Zondra," he said with a grim smile. "And, to my thinking, in the realm of chance and change,

"I CALL YOU TO STAND."

that is to say, the Kova."

"About this Brendar," she asked, her mind going to the combat training she lived by, "what is his skill level? Does he have experience in this 'stand' thing?"

Erique shrugged. "I have no idea; I have been away for a long time, you know. He is a few years older than me and has fought the Kreill and other clans in several battles."

"Who can I talk to about him? I will find out what his weaknesses could be."

"He has none," Cather said entering the bare stone room. She had been quiet for the finish of the evening meal before terms for the ritual were set and it was decided for it to occur at moonrise that very evening.

"Not possible," Arinna said with a sharp tone. "You of all should know that every man has a weakness. Or two!"

"Maybe in the lowlands," the tall Shoutte girl said with no acknowledgement of the intended irony in Arinna's statement. "No tested warrior of the highlands has any weakness; Zondra does not permit it. If he lives he has skill, there is no half measures in the highlands."

Arinna laughed and the tall woman stiffened, glaring at the redhead. "Have a care who you accuse of lying, tiny one."

"Tiny one?"

"Enough, you two!" Erique snapped. "She means no disrespect, sister, she has grown up on the fields of contention and you, Arinna, I told you Umbrians are proud and have great faith in the hands of Zondra. As they should."

The two women glared at each other and then turned their gaze to Erique, who had stripped his doublet and blouse so he wore only his kilt with the family crest of feathered dragon on it and a broad belt-girdle. His double-diamond-shaped brands stood out on his chest.

He stood tall with his breathing even and his manner untroubled. Now that he had set it all into motion, his nerves were strangely calm—thanks to his faith in Master Braphan's training and the truth of the Kova. He had learned to rob himself of worry, and simply enter into any endeavor as a problem to be solved, not an obstacle to be faced. And he also had learned to surrender the outcome to the Rythem. What would be would be as long as he did his best.

"Brother, why must you do this now? You have just come home." Her tone made it clear she feared the outcome of the contest could be fatal.

"You know why."

"Yes," she said. "I just wish…"

"You wanted to tell me something before the meal," he began to stretch and do his Old Kingdom style warm-up exercises. "What was it?"

She looked at Arinna then spoke in low tones. "Shadowcraft. Atrum was killed with 'craft and I believe someone in the stronghold called it down on him." She told him what had occurred on the night of their brother's death in great detail, how they found his twisted and blackened body, an empty husk drained of life, with a look of horror on his face. She had to pause several times from the intensity of the emotion as she recalled it.

The clerical student took a deep breath and nodded. "I suspected as much from what Davorna said. There were whispers of this in the eyes of so many at the meal. All the more reason for the clan to be united quickly before the other clans sense the divisions."

"Will your dying do that?" Cather sobbed.

"You have so little faith in me?"

"Zondra will not protect an outsider," she said flatly. "Especially with such an outland skill mark on his chest."

"Yulin protects the just," Arinna interjected. She stepped close to her friend and pointedly looked up at the Shoutte woman. "And my father taught him well."

Erique grinned at her statement. "Mind you," he smiled, "Arinna would never tell me my form was good under any other circumstances."

"How can you joke?" Cather rebuked. "Brendar will give no quarter. You have returned only to die the very same night and leave us with no leader still. And me with no brother at all."

"Sister," he said, his tone as serious as he could be, "I believe that Zondra will not desert Clan Shoutte. If I am meant to lead it, I will triumph and prove it to all. Even if I fall it is in keeping with my beliefs in the Kova, the principle of eternal change. I will have given my all and there will be no regrets. I believe the clan will survive even if I do not. And they will not follow me if I do not do this. Even you can see that I have no choice but to stand before them and prove my worth."

"Don't speak that way!" Arinna said. "If he kills you I swear he will not live ten heartbeats."

"No," he turned to her and said sharply. "You will promise to take no action; I don't doubt you would hack him like a fatted svor, but the clan would turn on you and you would fall. I promised your father you would return to him whole and hearty. I will not have him discomforted by my decisions."

"Discomforted?" She looked at him with wide eyes and hands on hips. "What about me? What am I supposed to do if you..."

"You will live, you will prosper." He turned to his sister. "Give me an oath that you will help Arinna return north, safely. She is here for me and should be untouched by this."

Cather and the redhead exchanged a look that was almost a challenge and the Shoutte girl reluctantly nodded.

The gesture seemed to relax him and then he turned once more to Arinna. "Please. I need you to do this; *a warrior does what must be done.*"

"I hate it when you quote my father's sayings to me." She was clearly working not to cry. She swallowed hard and then nodded. "What can I do to help? What is this ceremony?"

"To stand before Zondra and the clan," Cather explained. "One opens oneself to the hand of justice."

"I get that," Arinna said. "But what exactly does it mean? What are the terms? What weapons, the conditions? Are there prohibitions to certain blows or techniques?"

"The old ways were brutal," he said, as he went back to stretching on the floor. "Even by highland standards. The skin of a mountain goranga, like the one we saw, that furred beast native to the hills, is spread on the ground and each combatant is given a wooden shield and a crystal club. Only blood on that skin counts and both fight until one cannot rise or submits. There is little art, and no subtlety to the combat, only brutal aggression. Generally it is to the death, as few in the highlands ever submit."

"The contenders are allowed to change shields twice," Cather's voice was neutral to the point of sounding like a sleepwalker but her eyes, like Arinna's, looked ready to tear up. "No one on record has ever reached needing or being capable of asking for that third shield."

She turned to Erique and spoke in a hard whisper. "Please consider leaving now, brother. None will pursue you and you will be alive."

"To run away from combat?" he asked. "Not something I would expect to hear from a Shoutte."

"I have lost one brother. I do not wish to lose you."

"If I run, you will have," he countered. "I would never be able to show my face in the highlands again."

"But you will be alive. While you were away with your strange rites among outlanders you were still alive; I could imagine you, think to you, even talk to you when I needed to, like when we were little. But Brendar is a vetted warrior while you have spent your time studying singing and bone-setting. After he beats you to a pulp you will be dead and gone for real. Forever."

The tears came then and her shoulders started to shudder, but it was Arinna, not Erique who stepped to hold her. The clerical student lowered his head but continued stretching.

"Easy, Cather," Arinna held the taller girl. "Erique needs us to believe in him now. And I do; that matters. Belief! Do you who worship Zondra not believe in an afterlife?"

The taller girl sniffled and looked into the redhead's eyes. "Yes, the Caverns of Light."

"Then you know that death is not the end," Arinna said. "Only a change. Yulin tells me that and Erique believes in the constancy of change. So, know that if—and I say *if*—he were to lose he would not really be gone; just as your other brother is not really gone. As my mother is not really gone. And I have seen him fight; next to me he is the best student my father ever had. When he commits to combat, he is good as long as he tempers his tendency to be merciful. The Kovar students study the martial arts in minor from day one at the Academy; they can't spread the principle if they are dead, right? So he has had more than six years of solid training with weapons, strategy and focus. By the best instructors in all of Altiva. And *he* believes. Now *we* must believe."

The two women held each other, staring into each other's eyes for a long moment. Cather took a deep breath before she nodded. "I do not know your foreign ways, but they do not lack for courage. I will support my brother, for how can I have less faith in him than a little one like you?"

For a moment Arinna's jaw was tight then her face split into a wide grin. "See, not so strange, we little people from the far north!"

Erique stood then, his pre-combat preparations complete, and braided his hair to keep it out of his eyes when fighting. "I am ready now. It does my heart good to see you both at peace as I am. Let the ritual begin. To the Rythem!"

CHAPTER ELEVEN:
RITUAL

The great feast hall had been cleared and the tables moved to the sides of the vaulted, stonewalled room. A space in the center of the hall was prepared for the ceremony, circled with salt and blessed by the hold's resident priest of Zondra. Small fire pots dotted the circle at intervals to further divide the space from the mundane world and make it a sacred arena.

In the very center of the circle the skin of a mountain goranga was spread out. The furred beast, when alive, had stood almost twice the height of a grown man. Its white and red dappled pattern was a contrast to the deep green stone of the hall's floor.

Erique thought of the beast he had seen taken down by the tvek pack and the Shoutte riders and thought, *Brutal indeed, Arinna. It really is the highland way. Have I any real hope of changing this? Or should I?*

The entire stronghold's populace was crowded into the room, so that the normally cool hall was warm from the combined body heat of almost two hundred. The two galleries that lined the walls some fifteen feet up, where musicians usually played for gatherings were crowded with the kitchen staff. Only a few unlucky wall guards, still on duty for hold security, were not in the room to observe the contest.

None in the assembly wore even personal daggers out of respect for the ceremony; this was now a sacred space and only the two in contention. It was an old custom to prevent hot heads from disrupting the ceremony should the combatant they favor look to be losing. This was solely the province of the Duel-One to decide from this point forward.

The whole of the assembled crowd was solemnly quiet as the priest who, with three acolytes, lived in a small chapel in the hold, walked the outer ring of the circle. Each of the acolytes held a censer of herbs and prayed to invoke the justice of the dual-god.

When Erique, Arinna and Cather entered the room there was a quiet murmur that raised in volume when the crowd noticed the double-diamond brand on the clerical student's chest. There were murmurs of

"Blasphemer!" and "Outlander!" and many made the sign of Zondra in defense against such an outrage.

"I told you your skill mark would elicit comment," Cather said.

"I am not surprised," he said. "I would have been surprised if it did not, but I have nothing to hide, nor be ashamed of."

As the three stood at the edge of the salted circle, several people stepped aside to allow an older man with a balding pate and full white beard to step up to arm's length from Erique.

"It is really you, boy?" the old man said with a shaky voice. He reached out and his wizened fingers made contact with the clerical student's right cheek.

"Dundak," Erique greeted with a quiet voice. "Yes, it is I." He stepped forward to embrace the old man, all but enveloping him with his long, powerful arms.

"I was sure never to see you again, my student," the old man was near tears as he ran his hand on the shoulder of his old student. "Your brother would not even let us speak your name after you left us and had chosen that strange religion."

Erique smiled and he held the old man by the shoulders at arm's length. "I don't doubt it, but I never stopped remembering our talks, sir. So much of what you told me guided me to make that decision. There was so much wisdom in your words."

The old man gave a ghost of a smile. "I had always hoped so, heh heh. Those of the Age of Heroes fought dark forces to build the world as we know it and I saw in you the echo of their greatness. Your fists were always faster than your tongue, but I knew your mind was faster still. You fought then with fierceness but never with rashness."

"You always spoke in the training hall of the old days, before even the Mephan Invasion when there was questing for knowledge without fear," Erique nodded with a wide smile at the compliment. "You were always without the narrowness of so many others, teaching the full duality of Zondra and not the fear of all others."

"They respected me despite my failing eyes," Dundak said, "because my sword arm had been strong in youth; now that I am too old to fight, they endure me out of habit." He ran a hand along the shoulders and arms of the clerical student with a lifetime of warrior assessments and nodded. "Now they will have to respect you for the strength of your sword arm and the quickness of your mind. And the trueness of your heart."

"I hope, sir. I hope we may have many more talks to come when this is done."

"May Zondra permit. I will pray for you." The old war teacher stepped back.

"Who stands before?" the priest called in ceremonial tones that focused the attention of all in the hall.

"Erique of the Shoutte, I stand before."

"Brendar of the Shoutte, I stand before."

Erique's cousin was a decade older and half a head shorter but much wider than the clerical student, though none of that width was fat. His shirtless form showed the scars of many fights. His black beard was braided and his long hair hung free down his back.

"Zondra is the face of both justice and mercy," the priest named Ozam called. "To stand before them is to submit to their judgment. Do you still wish to stand?"

"I do," Erique answered.

"I do," Brendar agreed.

Kurvan stepped from the crowd and stood before the two men. "This is not a contest for leadership of Clan Shoutte," he said addressing the two men as well as the entire assembly. "Yet its outcome will have great effect, so think: do you wish to continue and is this in the best interest of the clan?"

"None will follow me if I back out, Uncle," Erique said. "And a stain on the courage of the Shoutte name would be unforgivable. It must happen."

"And none wish your outland ways," Brendar said. "I do this to purge them. I will proceed."

"So be it," the elder statesman looked to the priest who stepped forward to pass the censer between the two men.

"Let the judgment of the two aspects be final," the priest waved and two clansfolk brought round shields for each of the contestants. The round shields were wooden with a steel boss in the center, painted with the symbol of both Zondra and the dragon of the Shoutte Clan on them, wound around the edges. Each had a handle in the central boss for the combatants to grip.

Arinna accepted the shield for Erique, testing its weight and adjusting the grip of the boss on the reverse side of it.

Another clansman acted as shield aid to Brendar.

"I will pray to Zondra for you, brother," Cather said softly.

"And I to Yulin," Arinna added.

"To the Rythem," Erique whispered. His gaze was steady on his kinsman opponent.

The priest's acolytes stepped forward and held out the clubs to the two men. The weapons were three-foot long Ovar wood shafts, which thickened slightly toward the very end so the wielder's hand would not slip. The angular crystals that topped the clubs adhered to the shaft as if they had grown from them and seemed to glow from within as the crystal facets caught and reflected the torchlight from the room.

Each man took hold of the club and then ceremonially held it aloft for all to see. A murmur of approval went through the watchers as they did.

Erique exchanged a last look with Arinna, who changed her grim look to a grin and added a nod of encouragement.

Five drummers began to beat a rhythm and four young women began to sing a hymn to Zondra:

"Call up your courage, Summon your pain, Draw forth your weapons, For Zondra we praise, Drum of your heartbeat, Shrill of the pipes, If you strike hard victory's ripe, And if here in this circle, Your bodies must lie, If the cost of your triumph, Is that you must die, Then damn all tomorrow, And praise empty halls, For we raise tankards all, To the hero who falls!"

The priest waved and an under-priest acolyte struck a crystal gong.

The battle was joined.

Brendar charged, swinging the crystal-headed club with his full body weight in the blow, obviously intending to overwhelm and overrun his cousin in the first rush.

Erique had expected the charge by studying the bearded man's muscular tension and by knowing the battle mind of most highlanders. As the club sliced down at the cleric's head he dodged, deflecting the club with the edge of his shield.

He converted the power of the deflected strike on his shield to spin with his own club and send a horizontal slash at Brendar's waist.

The bearded man jumped back with surprising deftness for his bulk and, with a snarl of defiance, kicked at Erique's exposed right side.

The Kova student was struck in the hip and staggered left.

Brendar took advantage of the stumble and charged again to jam his shield hard into Erique's right side.

Cather—who had been holding her breath—gasped, but Arinna squeezed the Shoutte girl's hand she was holding to hush her. The redhead was watching the footwork of the two.

Erique took the energy of the shield rush to move away from the attack just as the crystal club smashed into his right shoulder. It was a glancing blow, but it opened a long red gash and brought an involuntary cry of pain from the clerical student.

The crowd all cheered. Arinna cursed, starting to step forward but Cather, still holding her hand, pulled her back.

As Brendar raised his club for a killing blow the Kovar spun to his left and sliced the edge of his shield into the bearded Brendar's middle. The older man grunted but slammed his own shield down hard on Erique's and at the same time swiped at the Kovar's face with his club.

Erique dodged back so that the razored clubhead missed his face by inches but the strike on his own shield was so hard it splintered the wood.

Erique dropped his broken shield and yelled "Shield!" But Arinna had anticipated this and tossed it to him so he was able to grab the handle in the steel boss in time to ward against a follow-up strike by Brendar.

The wound on the Kovar's shoulder was bleeding profusely now, the drops of blood staining the fur of the skin they were fighting over. Observers could see that his right arm was weakening, the club dipping down.

Brendar saw it as well and moved in to take advantage.

"He can't stay single," Arinna murmured.

Cather was about to ask what she meant when the clerical student tossed his shield intentionally at the legs of his cousin. When Brendar reacted by slamming his club down at the spinning disc Erique charged, now holding his own club in a two-handed grip.

Before Brendar could fend off the double attack, Erique had swing his club hard enough to splinter the bearded man's shield.

Brendar parried a second blow with a hard sweep of his club and called for another shield from his second.

"Hand Erique his other shield," Cather whispered to Arinna.

"No," the redhead said, nodding as she saw her friend assume a strong two-handed grip on his club. "He is good at Iskarian Old Kingdom style, with the double-handed grip on a sword and it will work for that weapon. With his weakened shoulders it is the right choice."

Brendar, rearmed with his new shield, pressed his attack again, but now Erique met his wild, sweeping smashes with barely moved deflections of the club he held in middle guard as if it were a sword. He gave ground slowly, but in a circular retreat so the two men stayed at the edges of the animal skin which was the only register of the violence that would count.

Brendar swung with increasing frustration as the slighter, younger Shoutte kept retreating, not responding to the fierce attacks save to deflect the strikes.

The watching crowd began to jeer as Erique seemed to be unable to reply to the vicious attack.

"Why doesn't he do something," Cather hissed. "To retreat is cowardice. He..."

"He is no coward," Arinna bristled then added with a grin. "He *is* doing something. A warrior picks his moment and his place. He is waiting for that moment. He about to make an idiot of the bearded bloat."

As she spoke the clerical student suddenly stopped so that his opponent, who had been almost at a full run in pressing his attack, was forced to come up short. Erique swung his club to beat Brendar's weapon down then jumped forward to kick the heel of his foot into the center of his cousin's shield.

The bearded man was off-balance enough that he dropped his club to try and balance himself.

Erique sprang forward again so quickly that it seemed between blinks and was abruptly standing with one foot on Brendar's right wrist and had the crystal club pressed against the fallen man's throat. The fallen man was almost dead center of the goranga skin.

"Cousin," Erique said. "I stand before Zondra and this assembly as winner; to take your life would be to rob the clan of your good right arm. Know that Zondra is the Dual One who is both strength and mercy. Will you force such a waste as to take your life to occur, or will you give me your allegiance?"

There was a stunned silence in the hall as all stared in disbelief at the scene before them. Even Arinna, who was gripping Cather's hand tightly, held her breath.

"Zondra has judged," Brendar said with a breathless exhalation. "You are Shoutte."

The murmurs in the room could not decide if they wanted to cheer or curse as Erique threw down his club and offered his hand to the fallen man. Then a cry of "Shoutte!" went up and all joined in repeating over and over, "Shoutte! Shoutte!"

"Yes!" Arinna yelled louder than anyone in the room and hugged a startled Cather. "I told you he was great!" The two of them moved to stand beside Erique. His old war teacher Dundak was smiling broadly and nodding his head.

The priest of Zondra tried to restore order by hitting the gong again, but the crowd surged forward to congratulate the two combatants.

That was the moment when the attack began!

CHAPTER TWELVE:

BLOOD WILL OUT!

Swordsmen burst onto the galleries above the hall and started slaughtering the occupants, either stabbing or simply throwing the helpless servants—men, women and children alike—over the railings to the floor below. Then invading archers sent flights of arrows down at the unprotected assembly.

The Clan Shoutte members below started to rush for the doors of the hall, but armed men appeared and hacked down the panicked and unarmed Shoutte clansfolk from the outside as they bottlenecked at the doors.

Cries of "Treachery!" and screams of terror filled the hall, mingled with the yells of the dying.

Arinna grabbed the last of the shields she had for Erique and got it up just in time to block an arrow that would have struck the clerical student.

"Get to the wall," Cather yelled to her brother as she grabbed his arm but he shook her off.

"We have to organize," Erique said. An arrow slammed into Brendar's leg but the burly highlander ignored the wound and pushed old Dundak down while grabbing his own shield up to protect the aged teacher.

"Erique," Arinna held the shield in front of the clerical student just as another arrow shaft slammed into it. "Get to cover."

"This was planned," he said with anger. His eyes scanned the room, taking in the details of room, the numbers and the positions of everyone, his mind speeding ahead to form a plan.

All around, arrows slashed into flesh, whistling down death from the galleries. The chaos of the slaughter, the screams of the victims, of mothers folding their bodies over their children to protect them and warriors at the doors screaming in angry frustration as they tried to fight their way out, barehanded against blades, echoed off the stonewalls.

None of the clanskin in the hall even had even personal daggers out of respect for the ceremony that had just occurred. They were trapped like svor to slaughter.

Erique concentrated on calming himself to see a clear solution. He called on all his priest-singer training to charge his lungs with air. The power that propelled his Priest-Voice, the most unique of all the attributes of the Academy Kova's training, had taken all of his years at the school to develop. It could heal or hurt or, as in this case, boom to fill a room like thunder.

"Clan Shoutte rally!" He sang with full power even as an arrow sliced into his left hip. His voice faltered only a note before Arinna jumped next to him to hold the shield to block two more shafts. He stooped and pulled the thick goranga skin up over his shoulders just as several more shafts thudded into it.

"They are deliberately targeting you," Arinna said. "They know you are the leader."

"Then I must lead," Erique said, before he took another breath, and continued with his call to arms. "Shoutte to the walls!" He sang at full power, "Use the tables as shields and ladders to make your way into the galleries!"

The quality of Priest-Voice was not just that its volume was loud enough to reach all the room, but also that the waves of sound were both above and below human hearing and thus reached into the very tissues of all those present. The song-order cut through the fear and indecision of all who heard—they were compelled to action. The clanskin raced to the tables and lifted the heavy furniture to create shelter for most of the occupants. Two groups of highlanders hefted tables at each end of the room to smash them into the intruding swordsmen at the doors.

When he had sung his order, Erique grabbed the arrow in his hip and snapped the shaft off a few inches from the skin.

"Get me up there," Arinna yelled to him with urgency as she, Cather and Erique moved toward the wall of the hall, all shielded by the animal skin as arrows continued to slam into it like a swarm of insects.

He looked at her in her leathers but without her usual rapier on her hip; she only had a dagger on her belt that she had smuggled into the ceremony. She saw his look.

"I have to get up there," she said. "I have all I need. I can't stay down here."

Erique nodded and acted at once, calling to his cousin Brendar. "Give me the shield," he ordered. The older man felt the compulsion of the command and raced over. "Together, cousin," Erique said, taking the edge of the shield the man offered.

Brendar surmised what the two friends were attempting to do and, though he looked incredulous, he complied.

The two men holding the shield crouched down.

Arinna backed off then charged, leaping onto the shield with both feet.

"Now!" Erique said.

The two men stood quickly and pulled up on the shield at the same time Arinna sprang. Using the momentum of the rising shield, propelled by the powerful arms of the cousins, the redhead flew up to the gallery as if on a rope.

Arinna reached the level of the railings soaring over them to slam into two of the archers. She screamed a warcry and set about smashing her shield edge into faces and slashing with her dagger at exposed throats.

At the end of the halls the doors had been barred and the Shoutte within the killing zone of the room were trapped against them.

"Take the tables as battering rams and get those doors open," Erique ordered his bearded cousin. He did not wait to see if Brendar obeyed, but turned and grabbed several other clanskin.

"Turn this over," he ordered a group of them huddling behind a table. He used full Priest-Voice and stood tall, throwing off the goranga skin in a gesture of defiance to the archers. "Up end it to use as a ramp!"

The group complied and leaned the upturned table against the wall on an angle. Erique took a running start and ran up the table like a springboard to launch himself to grab onto the bottom of the gallery railing.

Cather joined the group of clansfolk smashing another table into a barred door and after they broke through, raced out the doorway into the hallway. With the others she met the invaders in bloody hand-to-hand combat, the Shoutte clanskin grabbing weapons from the fallen invaders or using their bare hands as they overwhelmed the intruders with pure ferocity in the desperate struggle for freedom.

Arinna moved through the archers on the gallery, driving into them with the shield edge and slashing at their groins, throats or weapon's arms, then pushing them over the rail before most even knew she was there.

Erique came up on the gallery from the other end, pulling himself up mostly with his uninjured left arm only to confront an archer who pulled a short sword and hacked down at his head.

The clerical student dodged and, with an astounding show of agility, released the rail and grabbed the beard of the attacker—which had the effect of pulling the archer down to smash his throat into the banister.

ERIQUE...RAN UP THE TABLE...

Erique then climbed up over the choking man and took the sword from his slack hand.

By then the next archers had realized their position had been breached at both ends and some turned to face Erique while the others confronted Arinna.

"Late to my party, long legs?" Arinna yelled, as she ducked a short sword slash and drove her knife into the gut of one of the invaders, tearing up in a spray of gore.

The red-haired warrior was actually roaring with glee as she slammed into each archer, but they could not oppose her with more than two at a time on the narrow balcony and could barely swing their swords in the close quarters. They were all larger than Arinna, but she used this to careen from one to the other.

"You get too greedy, I was afraid you wouldn't leave any for me!" Erique called back, but then had no more time to quip. The clerical student used the short sword he had taken from his attacker with his left hand and took on each of the archers at his end of the gallery.

The highlanders fought with brutal aggressiveness but had none of the finesse Erique had learned from Master Braphan and his other instructors at the Academy. Most of the Umbrians, like Erique's cousin had done during the match, tried to overwhelm him with a rush but for all his size, he was as lithe and agile as Arinna. He let them attack then countered with either a deflection of their blade or a quick dodge that got him inside their wide swings, always with fatal results for the archers.

The invading archers in the opposite gallery, when they saw the dual attacks of Arinna and Erique, at first attempted to support their fellows by firing across the hall. That became pointless when the Shouttes down below copied Erique's improvised ramp. This meant that the clanskin began to swarm that gallery as well. This forced the archers on that gallery to fight the now furious Shoutte warriors to protect their own lives.

Soon fighting was going on both levels as the Shoutte clan members pushed out into the corridors outside both exits from the hall and back up onto the galleries. Bodies were thrown over the rails so that it soon seemed that death was literally raining down within the hall; those below grabbed any arms that fell and turned them on the invaders.

The tide had turned and soon the invaders on both galleries were all dead or dying.

"Head outside the hall," Erique called in full voice. "Take the stronghold back!"

Arinna raced up to him, now with a sword in her right hand and her dagger in her left. She was covered in gore and blood, most of which was not her own. "Where?" she asked. "I don't know this building."

Erique had a dozen minor cuts on his body, a bloody right shoulder and the arrow shaft protruding from his hip but his voice was steady and his gaze steely. "This hallway leads to stairs to the main floor. We can make it to the main gate that way."

He limped ahead of her out to the narrow corridor beyond the gallery and down a spiral stairs to the anteroom outside the hall.

The anteroom was already full of bleeding and dying men and women but more of the Shoutte were on their feet than the invaders.

"Clanskin to the walls," Erique called. "Shoutte to me!"

He charged through the hall with Arinna right beside him. Cather, herself covered in the blood of her enemies, joined them and the three led the charge out the hold to the courtyard where it was clear the main gate was still closed.

"Where are the guards?" Cather yelled, as they reached the entryway. "I don't see anyone on the walls."

"To the postern gate," Erique called and he veered to the hidden door that led down to the shore of the lake and could be used for sorties during sieges. It was normally kept heavily barred on the inside.

When they arrived at the postern, they found it open, the bar carelessly set aside in the corridor. They re-barred it.

"Organize parties to scour the stronghold and find why the guards did not see to stop this," Erique said to Kurvan, who met the three of them at the door. "Make sure there is no one else hiding here. Bring the wounded into the great hall." He turned to Arinna. "Get my healer's bag from my room."

"Erique," she said, "you have to take…"

"Me later. The clan first. I will be fine." He addressed his sister next. "Organize the clan to man the walls while we attend to the wounded."

"I will do that, Erique," Kurvan said. "Cather can deal with the bodies and the wounded."

"Good, thank you, clansman," Shoutte said. He sagged against the stone wall near the postern door, the weight of his wounds suddenly apparent on him. "We had better get back to the hall, Cather. Others will need me for healing."

"Come, brother." She put an arm under his and helped him limp back to the hall. "I will help you."

"We will do this together," he said. "Shoutte is strength."

CHAPTER THIRTEEN:
AFTERMATH

Clan Shoutte members had already begun to clear the dead from the great feast hall and Cather was quick to organize the tables as makeshift beds. Water was heated and bandages and other medical supplies brought.

Arinna returned with Erique's healer's bag and he set to boiling the powdered thodist leaves to use as a painkiller. He chose not to take any himself for his own wounds.

"Assess those who need me most urgently, Arinna," he told his friend. "You know this better than most."

"I will clean the wounds of those I can," Cather volunteered.

"Thank you, sister."

Erique was shaken when he saw that one of the seriously wounded was his old war teacher, Dundak, who he attended. The wounds of the old man were so serious that he could do nothing for him but give him some pain remedy.

"I go to the Caverns of Light," the old man said, as Erique held his hand. He had been struck by two arrows and had a bad gash on his head from a fall.

"I am sorry that…" Erique began.

"No sorrow, m'lord," the older man smiled. "You made me proud. I go to Zondra knowing I have at least one student who listened."

Then there was nothing anyone could do for the old man. Erique fought back tears and sang a low transition song for his old teacher as he turned to work on the other patients.

Erique, Cather and Arinna, along with an older woman, Leanna who was mid-wife for the clan, spent the rest of the night attending the wounded, of which there were forty. Another forty-four clan members had been killed in the attack, including three guards on the walls that had been attacked from behind.

Cather marveled at Erique's skill as he removed arrowheads and sewed up deep wounds, repairing as much as the limited instruments he had carried with him would allow. He also comforted those too serious for him to help, making them comfortable in their last moments. He sang softly as he worked, putting healing voice into the melodies. He was able to use some of Leanna's herbal stores to extend the antiseptic and medicinals he had available to help.

In addition to arrow and sword wounds, there were broken bones that needed to be set, impact wounds from clubs, and several of the children who had been traumatized emotionally by the horrors around them. It was to them that Erique gave a draught of calming medicine and sang a special song to ease their terrors so that soon they were in restful sleep, smiling as they dreamed of better times.

"You really are a healer," Cather said with quiet awe when he took a moment to lean against a table after stitching up Brendar's leg wound. The bearded cousin's wound was the last of the operations in a long night.

Erique smiled weakly, "I try."

The gruff, bearded former opponent evidenced confusion at the sudden change in his cousin. He said nothing but exchanged a look with Cather before he went back to guard duty on the wall as the stronghold was now on a full war footing with all guard posts tripled.

"Sit down, you big svor!" Arinna ordered Erique, pushing him into a chair and pulling up his kilt to get at the arrow still imbedded near his hip. She made a disgusted sound. "Fool, moving around has driven the point in deep, but you're lucky the fabric of the kilt kept it from digging deeper initially."

"Things needed to be done." He tried to stand but as he spoke his exhaustion was clear and she kept him seated with no effort.

"Well, if you have any thodist left, you better take it; I have to dig the point out."

"I used what I had. Go to it, I will be fine."

"Tvekdung!" she cursed when looking at the wound. "Cather, hold him, I don't want to cut anything useful in his hip." She took a crystal scalpel from his healer's bag that had been used and cleaned, and moved a glowgem closer to illuminate the wound.

The dark-haired Shoutte girl grabbed her sibling around the waist, pressing him into the chair as Arinna took the scalpel and opened the skin around the arrowhead.

"Don't move around, Erique," Arinna grinned. "If you make me slip you may have to adopt if you want an heir."

"Wait till I get you on the practice yard again," he said through gritted teeth.

Even though he tried to be stoic it was impossible for the clerical student not to react as the redhead sliced into his hip to open enough space to remove the arrowhead without ripping muscle.

She had to use crystal retractors to pull muscle out of the way and forceps to grasp the arrowhead. She had to work the tool gently to get the barbed point out of the flesh that caused Erique to grit his teeth. He blanched to deathly whiteness and hummed a healing tone to himself as she worked, almost passing out from the pain at more than one point.

When the arrowhead was all the way out, she dusted the wound with a cleansing powder that staunched the bleeding and then sewed the wound up.

"I'm not nearly as neat with the stitches as you or papa are," Arinna said, "but this will hold as long as you don't jump around too much in the next couple of days." She looked up and smiled at Cather's look of concern. "Oh, not to worry, tall hips, your brother won't listen to me anyway and will be dancing the khonal dance by tomorrow and ruining my lovely sewing work."

"You can let go now, Cather," he pointedly ignored Arinna's jibe. "I need to breathe to get back to my patients."

"I can see to those who are left, Lord," Leanna said. She was white haired but still vital and had an easy manner. "You should rest; you have done well here but the clan will need you to plan a counter-attack to this abomination."

"She is right," Cather said. "This can not go un-revenged."

"But who to punish?" Arinna queried.

"That may be hard to discover," Kurvan said, approaching the group. He gave a weary sigh and still had a smear of blood o his jerkin front. "The search party has scoured the whole building from towers to dungeons. The hold is safe with none hiding within. All those who attacked are dead, killed during the fighting. There were not any left to question—they at least fought to the last breath and showed that much honor despite their treacherous attack."

"And their clan marks?" Cather asked. "I had eyes only for their weapons during the fight."

"That is a confusion," Kurvan said. "There were Sween, Ranor, Kreill and unmarked bodies among them, with none in sufficient number to ascribe any major clan as the motivator to the attack."

"An alliance against us?" Erique attempted to stand but found himself too shaky and sat down heavily again as he became dizzy.

"I do not think so," the older Shoutte said. "If it were an alliance of other clans, then why so few attackers? There were not more than a hundred marauders. Any single clan could muster that many alone, so why bring in other clans or unmarked fighters into the fray? Why not overwhelm us with numbers?"

"Outlaws then, but why and to what end?"

"Perhaps they sensed a weakness here with you not yet confirmed as the Shoutte?" Arinna offered.

"Perhaps, but more important right now," Erique said. "Who let them in? They did not come in over the wall. The postern can only be opened from within."

"A traitor?" Cather realized with horror.

"It would have to be," Erique agreed. "The guards on the walls were too vigilant to allow any to scale them."

"Not in Clan Shoutte!" Cather insisted. "Not a traitor!"

"I know it is hard to imagine," Erique continued, "but what other explanation is there? The guards on the wall were surprised from behind, from within the hold. No clanskin would be so lax on duty as to allow an outsider to overtake them." There was a prolonged silence between them as each took in this possibility.

"What is to be done?" Cather finally asked in a tentative voice. She and Kurvan looked to the clerical student. When he shrugged, she added, "The others saw you in the ritual and if anyone still had doubt even in that, then they have seen you in real combat here last night. They will follow you into battle now with no hesitation. They no longer look on you as a weak outsider. You are Shoutte."

"Songs will be sung of your actions in the conflict here today, lord," Kurvan added. "But now your clan needs your orders."

Erique looked at Arinna who smiled at him.

"Well, 'lord,' what is next?"

He started to speak but she cut him off quickly, "Before you say anything, though, you need to rest and eat, or you will be useless to anyone. Remember my father says 'Decide with a fresh brain. You need rest.'"

"I agree, with her," Cather said. "You have had no rest at all, brother."

"It seems I am outvoted, Kurvan." His shoulders sagged and it was clear he had reached the end of his endurance. "I would have you put out word to all the clan and our allies. That will take a day to summon all. I will sleep as my wardens here demand in the meantime."

"Yes," Kurvan concurred. "That is the right thing. I will see to the guards and keep the gates closely watched."

Leanna spoke up now. "I will see to all here, Lord; take their advice to rest and have no care."

"Thank you, clanswoman," Erique said. "I surrender to female wisdom."

Arinna and Cather both helped Erique to his room in the keep. Arinna insisted he take to bed immediately. He sat on the edge of the bed and tried to bend forward to remove his boots but grimaced.

When Arinna knelt to grab his leg he protested, "I can take my own boots off."

"And open my best stitch work? Just be quiet, 'lord' and relax." She pushed him back on his bed and unlaced and removed his boots, tossing them aside.

He started to protest, but when he was horizontal all fight went out of him and he relaxed.

"Sleep, brother," Cather said.

"Yes," he whispered, "perhaps just a bit."

By the time she and Arinna had reached the door to the bedchamber, Erique was already unconscious and snoring.

"You need to rest as well," Cather said to Arinna, as the Shoutte girl eased the door closed. The two women were stood awkwardly looking at each other in the office of the suite.

Arinna, bandaged herself in a half dozen places, leaned against the bedroom door and looked up at the taller girl with a weary smile.

"Like you don't?" Arinna countered.

"I admit I am tired. But there are things still to do."

"One of those things is to set up a guard here for Erique."

"What do you mean?" Cather asked.

"If there is a traitor in the hold who let those brigands in," Arinna elaborated, "it seems likely that Erique is not safe, even here, since they targeted him in the hall. They were very deliberately trying to kill him at the beginning of the attack. The whole thing seems to really have been about beheading the clan, don't you think?"

Cather considered this, her expression darkening. "It is true; Atrum was killed in this very room. What can we do then, who can we trust?"

"I don't know," Arinna said. "I am going to set up my chair right here." The two women walked to Arinna's room where the redhead stripped off her bloody tunic for a new one and belted on her rapier. Cather stood by the door and watched the other woman while she changed.

"I will help you bring the cot to his office," Cather said. When Arinna paused in belting on the sword to look up at her the Shoutte girl added, "It will be more comfortable than a chair. I will then get some food and wine for us and bring a chair for me."

"For you?"

"He is not just my big brother, he is my lord. You and I can take turns napping on the cot while the other sits alert."

Arinna walked across the room and looked up at the dark-haired girl, her chin coming to just between Cather's breasts. "Well, let's get that wine and food then and see if we can find something to keep us awake."

CHAPTER FOURTEEN:
HIGHLAND RELATIONS

Erique slept through most of the day, waking just before twilight. He woke hungry.

When he opened the door to leave his bedroom to look for food, he was confronted by the sight of Arinna, seated on a cot outside his door with her back to the wall, with a sleeping Cather's head on her lap.

She looked up to the clerical student and smiled. "Good afternoon, sleepy head," she whispered. "Feeling better?"

"What is this? Another party I missed?"

"The outer door is barred," Arinna ignored his implication. "But we thought it best to keep an eye out, just in case."

He saw the bread and cheese on the desk near her and helped himself, washing it down with some juva ale. Between bites he said, "There should be funeral rites for the dead today."

"Yes," she said. "A messenger came by a while ago to tell us; at first sundown. We were going to wake you soon to see if you were up for it."

He limped to the window and looked out on the courtyard and the valley beyond. "There is so much wrong here, Arinna. I don't think I can help my people; my returning may have been pointless."

Arinna gently eased the sleeping Cather's head off her lap and came over to stand by her friend. "I admit there is so much I do not understand about your clan and this world, Erique, but I know you did not bring this on. This, whatever is happening, started well before you came; it is connected to your brother's death for certain, but there must be more."

"I know. I just feel overwhelmed by it all; my people need me to lead and to do that I must understand what is happening. And I have to admit that I do not." He turned to look down at her. "I disappointed so many when I left here for the Academy and thought I could forget it all and put it behind me. Now I have done it again. I've disappointed everyone at the Academy and come back here to this."

"Stop that," Arinna protested. "You did not disappoint anyone at the Academy, especially my father. I can't speak for anyone here, but no one can blame you for what is going on before you came back and last night you were the only thing that turned the battle for your clan last night. You, your thinking and your skill."

"She speaks truth, brother," Cather said, sitting up on the cot. Her hair was a tangle of snarls and her eyes sleepy, but her voice was steady. "I have never seen anything like how you and Arinna fought last night and I have seen many fights all my life. Battles. But nothing like how you took a certain slaughter and turned it into a victory. Surely the hand of Zondra was with the clan in the way you rallied them to the battle."

She rose and walked to stand by the friends, her right hand casually resting on the redhead's shoulder. Arinna reached up and squeezed it. "And afterward there are many of the clan who would have died from the wounds if not for your skill in saving lives as much as you had it taking them; even Leanna was amazed and she has nursed many a wounded fighter before. That is the dual deity for sure."

"Outlander skills," he said. "The same outlander skills that that provoked Brendar to cause me to Stand."

"But you did stand," she said, "And now all who witnessed that will not question you."

"Not now, perhaps, but again, as soon as I have an outland idea that clashes with some tradition. I will always be marked as an outsider."

"But now is when they need you, not in some imagined future. And you are exactly who they need," Arinna spoke up. "I know this is not my fight…"

He smiled, "I know you well enough; all fights are your fight."

"But,"—she made a face—"Cather is right. You can pull the clan together *now* and sort the rest out later. If you do not act there may not be a later for you clan."

He smiled at the two women and shook his head. "Outnumbered again."

"Even when I'm by myself with you," Arinna grinned.

"So, what is next?" Cather asked.

"I will need your help, sister, in learning more of what has been going on with the clan these last few years. Now I will get ready to attend the ceremony for the dead."

"I'll get the servants to send up heating stones and more food while you talk, *my lord,*" Arinna said with only a slight mocking tone. She walked to the door and slipped the bar off it. "And after you wash up, I have to look at that bandage on your hip to change it."

Erique ignored her taunting tone and went back into his sleeping chamber with Cather in tow. He poured some water in a bowl and used a crystal razor to shave while his sister talked.

"At first after Atrum took over from father, things stayed much as they were," she related. "There were incursions, of course, with the Sween and the Kreill clans testing the limits of our herds, but Clan Shoutte and our allies are strong enough that none would ever openly challenge us. Yet year after year the number of svor that went missing increased."

"A rise in goranga population?"

"We thought that at first," she said. "It does happen sometimes, or tvek packs if there is a dry season in the high meadows, but I went on hunts myself and while there were more than usual of the beasts there were not enough to account for the losses. Besides, they would leave bones or skins even if they dragged their kills to some cave. We never found any signs of the svor that went missing, neither tracks or remains."

"So, thieves?"

"Yes. And at the councils the other clans often—too often—spoke up against us. The fear was not there."

"Fear is no way to rule," he removed his bloody kilt and set to cleaning what wounds he could reach, his stiffness from sleep and soreness from his wounds making it a slow process. "It is ultimately self defeating and thus a short-lived means."

"How then?" she asked, puzzled.

"Respect," he answered. "Father was powerful, but the other clans knew he was just as well; that is always the way. Fear can be overcome; anger is strong, hate is stronger. But respect, like love, can stand above all."

His sister looked at him with a stunned expression as Davorna and Arinna entered with a woven basket that held the heating stones for him to use in his bath. The women went directly to the built-in stone trough on one side of the suite and, using crystal tongs, slipped the glowing stones into a reservoir for them in the channel above the tub. In the same way that glowgems retained light for hours after exposure to any light at all, the grown crystal heat stones absorbed, magnified and dissipated heat for a long time after being heated in a fire.

Davorna opened the sluice to the tank of water on the roof of the tower and water flowed over the stones, heating as it did.

"The other clans will sense weakness if we act any other way than a show of power," Cather began.

"No, sister. Skill and strength earn respect; true kindness can come only from strength. It is the obligation of the strong, because, sister, the world changes and the strong become weak someday and they will need the good will of their former kindness. "

"I left the food in the office," Arinna said. "Avrum steaks, greens, some kulva bird breasts and some fish I didn't recognize. And fresh bread. I almost ate it on the way up."

"You seem to talk about food all the time," Cather remarked.

"Except when she is shoving it in her face," Erique chuckled. "She can eat my weight on a daily basis." He eased into the tub, wincing when his wounds came in contact with the hot water.

Arinna looked hurt. "I am very energetic," she said, then shot a look to Cather. "Or hadn't you noticed?" The dark-haired Shoutte girl colored pink and Erique laughed.

The old servant watched the interplay between the three with hooded eyes, obviously uncomfortable in the presence of the outsider. "Will that be all, Lord Shoutte?"

"Yes, thank you, Davorna. I will see you at the ceremony."

After the woman had left and Arinna returned from barring the outer door again, Erique spoke.

"So strange to be called that, really called that."

"Lord Shoutte?" Arinna said, this time with no taunt in her voice.

"Yes. It was my father. Then it was Atrum."

"Yes, and now it is you," Cather said.

"Not completely till I sit vigil," he said. "But even the thought of it is … strange."

Arinna stripped off her doublet and without being asked, knelt by the tub and began to scrub Erique's back, a fact that took Cather by surprise. When she saw the look on the taller girl's face Arinna smiled. "There are so many times after a training session that we can't even raise our arms to wash that we got into this habit; I have the worst of it, as he has more surface area to scrub."

Erique ignored her and asked, "Sister, you spoke of things in the clan becoming odd…"

"Yes," Cather said. "After the herds began to have losses, some of our shipments of nekot to the coast disappeared en route."

"Outright disappeared?"

"Yes, with no one who was accompanying them ever heard from again."

"Any idea what clan is behind it?" Arinna asked. Erique waved her off and stood shakily in the tub. His wounds were angry red, but had not reopened.

"No," Cather said. "We have some word that other clans have had losses as well, but, of course, none of them will trust us enough to confide anything they know."

"We had some words with the waystation on the road to Westral City," he said. "They said that few caravans went through last season and none from this season. From any clan."

"So it is true," Cather said. "They have had the same troubles?"

"So it would seem. And then Atrum died by shadowcraft," Erique donned a robe and walked to the door. "And now we must be concerned that there is a traitor amongst our midst."

"Yes," his sister said.

Arinna removed the rest of her clothing and then moved to unfasten Cather's belt.

"Arinna!" the Shoutte girl said in surprise.

"We need to be clean for the ceremony, right?" the redhead said. "No reason to waste the warm water." She removed the rest of the stunned Cather's clothing and pulled her toward the tub.

"I'll save you some avrum," Erique said, "but I can't promise on the kulva breasts so don't be too energetic."

CHAPTER FIFTEEN:
CALL TO VENGEANCE

The dead of the Clan Shoutte were arranged on pyres along the shore of the lake that Stormrest jutted into. There were now forty-eight bodies, some of them only children, the corpses cleaned and dressed in their finest.

The retainers and outriders of the clan and all the close allies that could make it to the ceremony had gathered so that there were nearly five hundred live souls arrayed along the shore of the ice-cold water as the smaller, faster, sun began to set.

Erique was dressed in kilt and wore a red shirt which was opened at the chest to reveal his double-diamond skill brand scars. He wore his saber on his hip though the pressure of it rubbed enough against his wound that he had to adjust it to wear on his right side instead. Everyone at the ceremony was also armed, as it seemed on the minds of all that violence was to follow. There was fear of an attack at any moment, with lookouts placed at the far edge of sightlines so nothing could be left to chance.

Kurvan stood on a stone outcropping that was raised above the shore of the lake with the priest of Zondra standing beside him. The old man had survived the night's attack due to Erique's tending.

Arinna wore a borrowed green dress shirt and her leather riding trousers, with her rapier resting familiarly at her side. She stood beside Cather; both women stayed behind Erique who stepped between Kurvan and the priest. They were as much watching the crowd for danger as they were there in case the strain of the ceremony became too much for him.

"The clan awaits you, kinsman," Kurvan said in quiet, solemn tone.

The old priest of Zondra, Ozam, leaning on a walking stick and his chest heavily bandaged, added, "They will hear the words of the presumptive Lord of Shoutte before this ceremony." He looked at the clerical student with new eyes but there was still suspicion in his glance.

"Afterward we must prepare the vigil," Erique said. Then he exchanged a look with Arinna who grinned encouragingly at him so he took a deep breath and addressed the gathering.

"Clan Shoutte and all who align with us," he spoke in a full voice that boomed across the lake to echo from the rocky cliffs on the far shore. "I did not sit The Vigil yet but in this time of crisis I stand here as advisor-elect to you all. I will sit that vigil later. We all know is not a time to show weakness, yet as much as our hearts cry out for vengeance the question is, from whom do we ask this vengeance?"

Cries from the crowd of "The Sween," "Ranor" and other clan names came up till the chorus of shouting was deafening. He let it build for a while then held up his hand for silence, which stopped them with expectant expressions.

In the pregnant quiet that followed his voice was soft yet firm and reached all on the lake shore as if he were speaking directly to each of

"THE CLAN AWAITS YOU, KINSMAN," KURVAN SAID...

them. He put calming Priest-Voice underneath it all so it touched them deep in their hearts. "Hold, clanskin! The intruders were of many clans and a number even unmarked; they were outlaws who have somehow organized! We must guard against them and root them out at the same time. This we can not do alone; our wounds are too fresh and the enemy too scattered."

"What will we do?" A cry came from the crowd.

"I will send riders to the other clans and call for Parley."

"Parley?" a number of the crowd cried. "No, we have to attack!"

"Attack whom?" Erique replied. "Would you have us attack the Sween and the Ranor, and how about the Kreill? We certainly cannot leave them out. What then? All the unaffiliated clans and families? How many warriors would we face? Hundreds? Thousands? More? And how many are we? And how whole are we as a fighting force?"

He paused and surveyed the faces staring up at him. "Look at all of you. Look to your neighbor on your left and right; memorize their face for they may die if we follow that course. Certainly many of them; no matter how well they fight, can each defeat ten, twenty, fifty other fighters? If we attack them and they have not done this, we will be in the wrong; Zondra will know. Yet if we enlist them, if we clans can work together as we did when the Mephan Empire tried to lay hands on our land, we can defeat any outlaws. It was done in our grandsire's time and it can be done again to face this menace within that is easily as great as any invasion from without."

A murmur of comments went through the crowd as all present debated with reverent tones the proposition he had placed before them.

Erique looked to Arinna and beyond her Cather, and both women nodded. Kurvan, his expression implacable during the speech even gave a grim smile.

After a time when the murmurs died down, the gathering looked up silent again and waited for the clerical student to speak once more.

"I direct that our Uncle Kurvan send out word to the other clans after we have concluded this ceremony. Then I will sit vigil with my brother that Zondra may visit wisdom upon me and we may find justice for him and for our slain clanskin." He paused for a moment then called out the family motto. "Shoutte is Strength!"

All there returned the cry. "Shoutte is strength!" echoed across the lake like a hymn of power.

When the chant finished, Erique looked to the priest at his side and nodded. The prelate signaled to under-priests who began drumming the dirge for the dead. The drummers began the song and soon all the voices on the shore of the lake joined in and all sang the traditional send off song of the clan.

"*Circle cast round, Blood on the ground, Summoning, dark and cold, cry to the night*

"*Invoke the fright, now as in days of old. Hallowed this eve, for us who grieve, for our brothers and sisters who've passed, the veil now is thin, and the darkness within is revealed in its glory at last.*

"Let my death be clean, Let my death be quick, Let me not grow old, Or linger with the sick, Let there be true meaning in my final fall, let those left behind, be free of the tyrant's thrall. Let me lead to land of joy and rest, let me die a free and a warrior's death."

When the song finished, the pyres were all lit and the perfumed corpses of the clan's dead moved to join their ancestors in the Caverns of Light above the sky with the memories of those left behind. Erique, whose voice was loudest and clearest of all those who sang, walked from the speaking rock and went back toward the hold, showing a slight limp but without peaking another word. He ignored questioning looks from many, including a grim-faced Cather and a stoic Arinna. Kurvan walked with Ozam, helping the old priest as they went to prepare the ceremony that would have to follow for the vigil.

The others walked slightly behind Erique all the way to the stronghold gates, aware of the suddenly confused looks around them. The adrenaline rush of the cheer left the crowd with their thirst for vengeance unsatisfied.

The clerical student seemed to take no notice, his head high, his expression set. He continued straight up to his suite in the keep, all but ignoring comments from both women until he was in the office.

Cather grabbed his arm to turn him around. "Answer me, brother, why did you do that?"

"What else could I do? We are not strong enough to attack every clan in the mountains and there would be no point. It must be as clear to you as it is to me that it is some outlaw group. The other clans have to be having the same problems and despite what Arinna may think, I believe we highlanders can cooperate. It has been done before and it must be done now."

"If there is someone in this building who helped those killers get in here," Arinna said, "they will find a way to stop you talking to the other clans. You have to realize that."

"They can try," Erique smiled. "But now I must go and sit with Atrum in the Eye of Zondra, after I change."

"Eye of Zondra?" Arinna asked.

Erique took off his dress clothes and donned a long robe while Cather explained, "The room below the hold where our brother's body lies unchanging from the moment we found him dead."

"It is a natural crystal fresh bowl of sorts where the line of the clan leaders lie in state for eternity," Erique said. "It is in a deep cavern, the reason this stronghold was built here generations ago. I will sit with him and the others and ask for the wisdom of Zondra to lead the clan well as the other Shoutte leaders did."

"Sitting with the body all night?" Arinna's expression showed distaste for the idea. "What will you do there?"

"Sing to Atrum," he said quietly. "As I could not sing to him when he was alive."

+++

The three companions walked back down through the keep in silence. All of those they met, aware of his destination, made the sign of Zondra with quiet reverence. There was less suspicion in their glances now, many owing their lives to the clan head-elect. Now there was a pride in their glance, a curiously hopeful look. Some even chanced a smile at the heir.

Stone stairs led into the bowels of the stronghold, down below the kitchens and dungeons to the point where the walls of the corridors were crudely hand hewn from the naked rock, a natural narrow passage widened by the hand of many generations of Shouttes before.

At the bottom of the stairs, in a wide grotto, the old priest of Zondra, Ozam, two acolyte under-priests, Kurvan and three other clan members greeted them. They were standing before a large brass-studded, steel-banded door of ovar wood with the symbol of Zondra etched on it.

"Do you come to sit vigil in the Eye of Zondra, Erique of the Shoutte?" the priest intoned formally.

"I do, reverend," Erique replied. "By my right of birth, my devotion to the clan and my hope for the guidance of Zondra I come to sit vigil with the Shouttes of Shoutte past."

"Then enter and commune with Zondra and the essence of the Shoutte before you and all the Shouttes of the bloodline before them," the priest waved toward the entrance of the vault-like door.

Erique gave a look to his sister and Arinna and then moved forward to the door of the vault.

"I go to do my duty to the clan," he said aloud in the formal phrase that began the ritual. "Shoutte is Strength!"

The under-priests, male and female, opened the heavy door and Erique dropped his robe to stand naked before the entrance before he stepped through into the dimly lit, crystal-walled room. Kurvan accompanied the clerical student up to the opening of the vault and stood in the doorway.

"Courage," the older man advised quietly as he stood by him, facing into the vault. "Shoutte is strength! Be Shoutte."

Then the door of the vault was closed and barred behind Erique and he was alone with the corpse of his murdered brother.

CHAPTER SIXTEEN:
THE VIGIL

After the door to the crypt closed, the under-priests slid a bar across it and took up positions on either side of the door, ceremonial staves in hand. Kurvan made the sign of Zondra and then stepped over to Cather.

"Your brother does us all credit, Cather," the elder Shoutte said. "He makes one proud to be Shoutte."

"Yes, Kurvan," she said. "He is not the boy who left here. He has returned a man. I think, perhaps the very man the clan needs at this time."

"What now?"Arinna stood barely coming to the shoulders of any of the others but if she was discomforted by this she did not show it.

"The under-priests will monitor the door that none may disturb the vigil," the old priest said in a very tired voice. He leaned heavily on his staff, his wounds from the previous night taking their toll. "When the Elder Brother is above the horizon we will open the door and Shoutte will have a new leader in all respects and with no doubts."

"Do we have to wait here?" The redhead asked with a glance back up the passage to the hold.

"No," Cather said. "I should see to making sure that the wounded are cared for and their children fostered; we are one family."

"So we can get some food then?"

Cather looked down at the redhead with a shocked expression. "You really are always hungry."

"So?"

+++

The sound of the crypt door closing behind Erique echoed off the crystal walls of the burial chamber of The Eye of Zondra with the force of thunder. The chamber was the size of the great hall, a natural cavern whose irregular walls were studded with crystals in such an array to create the natural 'fresh bowl' condition. The effect was that all organic matter within the cavern stayed forever un-decayed.

Long ago it was the reason the Shoutte clan built its stronghold above the space and why it had become the burial vault for all the generations of Shoutte leaders. The whole area was lit by two tripod-held glow gems on either side of the vault door. The tripods cast a dim green light and had been charged in the sun's light to last for the length of the deathwatch.

The cold flagstone floor was damp as the barefoot cleric moved forward into the room.

The body of Atrum lay in his best robes on a carved crystal table twenty feet in from the crypt door. Beyond his brother, further in the cavern at the edge of shadows, Erique could see the bodies of ten generations of Shoutte leaders, male and female, on tables.

Each of the leaders were in their death robes, looking exactly as they did when they had been placed in the tomb. A few were withered from sickness or old age but most had died violent deaths, some barely into adulthood, for the highlands were a demanding and dangerous domain.

Erique felt a sudden inner chill as he approached the body of his brother. His steps slowed, his bare feet feeling as if they were weighted. He could only move with conscious effort.

The elder Shoutte's face was still contorted in a rictus of horror, his blue eyes wide, his skin blackened and drawn tight so he looked to have died twenty years older than he actually did. Erique could not even imagine what terror could be so great as to frighten his brother and blacken and desiccate his body in such a way.

"You were always the brave one," Erique said in a quiet voice to his brother. "So fearless in the training yard and on the raids; even not afraid to brace father when you felt you were in the right, Atrum. I know you didn't believe it, but I did look up to you even when I chose to leave I looked up to you and thought always you were the one to steer the clan when I heard."

Erique knelt by the head of his brother's body, reaching a hand up to touch the cold, blackened skin of Atrum's forehead. "I never would have left if I did not think you could take over the clan when father d-died—though as strong as he was it seemed like he might live forever and I never had a doubt about you taking over. You were ready as anyone here could be."

He smiled, not even bothering to fight the stutter. "T—t-here you have it, older b-brother, the Principle of Eternal Change in action. See why I was drawn to the K—k-Kova? Not that I wanted to turn my back on anything here, but you have to understand I never saw what my place could be here, brother, I mean, you were b-better at numbers and tougher than me, a full ten years older and Cather was a better fighter and runner than me, at least back then. All father would ever need to help him. All the clan would ever need. I always felt ... extra. Uncle Etrar was the only one who ever made me feel really special. I suppose, at first that was why I decided on the Academy. B-b-before I came to see the beauty of the Kova. It was a chance to be part of something and matter."

Erique laughed, the sound of his voice echoing oddly off the crystal walls, then took a deep breath and concentrated to suppress the stutter. "You don't need to hear my troubles, though, eh? You have troubles of your own ... or had. You should be sitting happy in the Goldern Caverns, eh, all the troubles of the Clan behind you now. Your transition was hard and I know you must have suffered, but you are beyond that now. At least I hope so. But how? How did it happen? And why? And who? I promise you, brother, I will find out. After that I honestly do not know that I can take up the burden of the clan to shoulder it the way you did. I just am not the man you were; I am barely a man at all even though you were only a few years older than me when you became The Shoutte. No one here really thinks I am a man and, and I am so very unsure. All I know for sure is that I believe in the Kova and I wish I could have sung for you in life. I would have liked to gift you that, brother. It is all I have."

He looked at the face of his dead sibling and recalled all the times as children when his older brother was the icon he and Cather chased around, trying to be part of the 'big kid' games. It made him smile at the memories.

As the night wore on in the sepulchral space, Erique sang many truth chants to his brother's body and the corpses of his ancestors but the time wore heavy on him. It caused him to reflect on all that had happened in his time back in Umbria. He imagined his brother in that same ritual, kneeling before their father's body but without the conviction of the Kova to comfort him.

"You were never patient, Atrum. I think this must have made you almost mad with frustration." The thought of his solemn brother irritated by having to spend a whole night in inactivity made Erique smile and then he felt a little guilty for it. "I know it was hard for you, big brother, yet you rose to shoulder the burden of the clan and administer it well. And learned patience and were a good chief. I thank you for that."

After a time he began an old highland song that he knew his brother had liked all the years before when they were children and which, back then, he could not have sung at all let alone with the depth of Priest-Voice in it he could now.

"Life stealer, blade of my enemy, sharper than my mortal pain, gore soaked yet hungry, come to me with blessed peace, A razor sharp rapture and release. My sword thirsts for blood edged to sup'on thee which of us will be set free? Fire, fury, axes red, the living always envy the dead—warriors calling We who wield steal, Ne'er to surrender, Ne'er to yield.

Called to the Caverns of Light with Zondra above, whatever the odds drink enemy blood, All we desire is one last caress of a warrior Goddess we all call Death!"

Then Erique cried for a long time for his brother, for himself and for the clan he hoped he could help but was sure he could not.

While he cried, he failed to notice the pool of darkness near the bodies of the past Shoutte leaders. The black spot began to grow and coalesce. At first it was only a shadow and then it moved directly toward the kneeling man!

CHAPTER SEVENTEEN:
THE LIVING DARKNESS

Erique suddenly became aware of an indefinable presence in the crypt. He neither heard anything nor felt anything physically, save that the room seemed to become colder, yet some inner senses alerted him to the presence of 'the other' in the space with him.

He turned to see the tendrils of darkness moving slowly across the room in his direction. A flowing, inky blackness—like oil in water but swirling and viscous—moved through the air directly at him.

The clerical student was paralyzed with the sudden shock of it and stopped his song of life in mid-note. He knew in a heartbeat that he was staring at the thing that had killed his brother, and more—he knew he was looking at something outside of the reality he lived in or had ever heard of. A force of darkness that was inherently evil.

This was beyond crystal-craft or warp-craft. This was something older, primal. It was some rift in reality that had been summoned into his reality and was antithetical to it, perhaps to all living and breathing things. It was shadowcraft of the darkest, most primitive form from a time even before the Mephan Invasion of old.

It was a primal force, perhaps from a time before time, a swirling, bubbling mass of non-existence that clawed at his being and insinuated itself into his mind and soul and intruded into the now from the no-time of the before times.

He tried to will himself to move, to rise off his knees and back away from the encroaching Stygian darkness, but his muscles were frozen, locked in place as the ebony darkness oozed toward him. The deep, sudden, cold in the vault sliced into him like a knife and he shivered uncontrollably.

The blackness was more intense than anything he could imagine, so dense and dark that there were levels within it, layers of ebony that were so absolute that the void within the blackness reached out for him.

I will die this way as Atrum did if I do not act.

Yet the muscles of his arms and legs would not obey his mind. The tendrils of dark slithered to him, crawling over his limbs and up his body with liquid progression.

I have to act or I will die, or worse.

He felt the cold leeching to his very soul, dripping like liquid night into his eyes and mouth, flowing into his nose and ears to fill him, throttling his throat as if it was a clawed hand from beyond a primordial era. It ripped into who he was and had been all his life until it touched the core of his beliefs, his adherence to the Kova.

The blackness penetrated deeper than anything else in his life except The Way of the Kova. It had been the way that had filled him and displaced all the doubt and pain of his youth, all horror and uncertainty of his upbringing, for it gave logical strength to it all. With the Kova he saw that the changes, good and bad, were all part of the grander plan; he accepted that and it gave him comfort to endure and even prosper no matter what he had faced so far in life.

So as the primal cold of the living darkness wrapped itself around his soul, Erique reached deep into the years of training and devotion to pull forth a truth chant, a song of pure hope, from his deepest memories.

The notes began in a minor key, soft at first, but then the melody grew as the notes linked together to swell and fill his chest with air and his throat with voice, and finally fill the air around him with song.

The sound that came from his mouth staggered into existence at first then danced and spun, pushing back at the blackness that pressed in and around Erique. The vibrations of the song reverberated off the crystals of the vault walls to amplify the notes and slam against the darkness like an ebb tide of the ocean.

It was only a collection of notes at first, ruptured and broken, but as he concentrated, his muscle memory and determination took over and a song was born. It formed around his desperation and shaped into hope to become a remembered chant, a hymn to his belief and his reality.

The crystals in the walls of the vault began to glow with the reverberating sound of the song, a song of life and light that battered at the darkling force that was assaulting the clerical student as he fought for not just his life, but his very sanity and his eternal soul.

+++

"Another helping?" Cather asked Arinna as the redhead filled her plate again with avrum steak. She had already downed two helpings and was washing all down with the highland version of juva ale.

"Of course," Arinna said. The two women were seated in a quiet corner of the kitchen while the activity of feeding the visitors to the hold went on. The main hall was still being used for the wounded, so tables had been set up in odd corners of the kitchens and halls.

The kitchen help did their best to ignore the two but cast a number of covert glances at the tiny red-haired stranger, still not sure how they felt about the ferociously eating little warrior woman despite her actions against the invaders.

"Do you think about anything but food and fighting?" the Shoutte girl asked, as she passed another full plate to Arinna.

The redhead gave a lop-sided grin and stared into Cather's eyes. "Really, you have to ask that? After I have eaten I can show you what else I like to do."

Cather blushed. "I mean…"

"Excuse us, dames," a male voice drew the attention of the two women. It was a young man not much older than Cather, with features that spoke of kinship. His dark hair was cut short and his upper lip was attempting to grow a mustache. Behind him were two other Shoutte retainers in kilts who, like him were wearing highland swords. "I apologize kinswoman, but we wanted to speak to the visiting warrior, if we may."

"It is alright, Turar," Cather said. "What is it?"

"I uh, I was there in the hall last night," he said addressing Arinna. "Though Javick and Thorvin were not. They do not believe my description of how you fought, dame."

Arinna grinned, looking from Cather to the three young male faces. "Oh?" She cut another piece of avrum and soaked it and some bread into the gravy before popping it in her mouth. While she chewed, she added, "So how can I help you?"

The young boy looked to the others and swallowed. "We were wondering if you had time to show us some of what you did? I have never seen such swordplay. The way you moved was amazing, how you dodged and cut…"

"You are making it all up," the one called Javick said to Turar with a sneering tone. He had his long hair braided into a single plait and was broad shouldered and long limbed, with a high forehead and sharp cheekbones. His clan kilt was girdled with an ornate, studded belt from which hung a highland sword and a small shield that both looked like they had much use.

"It is pure fantasy. No one can move like that with a sword, especially this little thing and her little needle poker."

This caused Arinna to laugh and Cather to gasp in horror.

"All is fine," Arinna pushed the plate away from her, wiping her lips on her sleeve. "Why don't we go to your training yard?"

Cather looked at the smaller girl with shock. "Arinna, this…"

"We do not mean to inconvenience you, dame…" Turar apologized.

"No inconvenience, sirah," the redhead's face lit in a predatory smile. "I need to work off this meal and some nervous energy while I wait for Erique to emerge from his rock cocoon." She looked over at Cather and added, "One way is as good as another."

The three boys led the women out of the kitchen past the ovens to a small side yard where racks of wooden weapons were stacked under a shed. There were practice pells and throwing targets set up at the opposite end of the long, narrow space.

Arinna burped loudly when she reached the center of the space, turning to face the other four. "Well now," she she drew her rapier and held it up as if presenting it. "This is a Cozen-style rapier, modeled on the old Mephan swords but with better steel and, obviously, forged to fit my frame."

"Small, you mean," Javick, who was also the tallest of the three Shoutte clansmen, snickered.

Arinna prickled but her grin widened. "Why, yes, it is smaller though of a length that clumsy highland hacking tool you have at your side, but thinner and, uh—more agile, sirrah."

"Arinna," Cather warned, seeing the smaller girl's posture change. "Don't…"

"Not to worry, Cather, dear," Arinna said, with a calm voice and a soft laugh. "Just like a lesson in my father's yard." She resheathed her sword and removed her belt, handing them to Cather.

"Now, sirrahs," she invited, "who would like to show me how your highland swords are correctly used against—uh, smaller opponents?"

CHAPTER EIGHTEEN:
Lessons

The three Shoutte clansmen looked from one to the other when Arinna opened her arms and smiled invitingly, repeating, "Come on, which of you will show me how to use those dinky things on your hips against my tiny body?"

The three reached to draw their blades but Cather spoke up. "Training swords," she called.

"No," Arinna objected with a grin. "They never have the same weight and heft as one's own personal weapon and I would be remiss as a teacher if I allowed that."

"But Arinna…" Cather began.

"We have no wish to harm you, dame Arinna," Turar was suddenly unsure about his request for an exhibition.

"I knew you were lying about how she fought," Javick said. "She is asking for real blades so you will fear to hurt her and hold back."

That made Arinna laugh again. "Oh, no reason to hold back, tall one, unless of course, the Shoutte sacks are empty decorations swinging between your legs."

Javick made a snarling sound and launched himself at the redhead, drawing and swinging his short sword in a blow that was intended to cleave her in half from skull to groin.

"No!" Thorvin called but the tall figure had already charged, his blade slicing straight at the smaller outlander.

Thorvin need not have worried, for Arinna was no longer standing where Javick's blade passed, having nimbly danced aside, moving almost as if the blade was moving in slow motion.

"You see, the cutting edge is a lovely thing," she said as she avoided a second slash at her midsection. "But it takes longer to slash than thrust and the movement is announced ahead of the attack if one keeps an eye on the tension in the shoulder." This prompted Javick next to stab at her with the broad blade, but she hopped back so the thrust fell short.

She slapped the flat of the blade out of her path with the palm of her hand and stepped in to poke a finger into his chin.

"Plus," she continued as she retreated before he realized she had touched him, "Footwork is the key to all of it. One must be both stable and nimble. In your case your footwork is terrible; you are putting yourself off balance with each swing, overextended by trying to use too much power to do the job. Not every blow should be intended to cleave a tree in half. Especially such a small twig of a tree like I am."

The tall boy made a strangled sound of annoyance then swung three more times with Arinna avoiding each slash or thrust with seemingly little effort. She literally danced around the swordsman until Javick's frustration stopped him, near tears.

"See," Turar said with a broad smile to his friend. "I told you she moved like nothing I had ever seen."

Arinna accepted the compliment with a grin but stepped up and put a hand on Javick's sword arm. "Footwork really is the key, my friend. The size or type of weapon does not really matter, rapier, Old Kingdom sword or your highland cutlass, it is all in the footwork, warrior. Even with your superior reach it was your footwork and your weight shifts that warned me where you were going to attack; there are only certain angles each attack can come from, especially with that particular type of weapon."

She proceeded then to show the taller boy what he had done wrong, step by step. The others listened with rapt attention. She corrected his footwork, showed him how to keep centered and extend his reach with his strides for any attacks.

When she had them bring out the wooden practice wasters and shields, they all, including Cather, settled into a more formal class by moon light. Though they had all had war classes in the hold, it was nothing like the reasoned and studied combat practices of the Kovar Academy training which was acknowledged as one of the most proficient on the northern continent, possibly in all the world.

Arinna was able to point out and correct many of the weakness of the four fighters, easily falling into a teaching style she had learned from her father, encouraging and correcting with gentle humor and perfect form as example.

By the end of two exhausting hours the three clansmen were almost as enamored of Arinna as Cather was. When all five stopped at last for water they were laughing and amazed.

"We will be the scourge of the clans with what you have taught us, dame!" Javick seemed almost proud to have been defeated by her, certainly feeling no shame to 'lose' to so proficient a warrior.

"You are probably that already," Arinna laughed. "At least in the sleeping quarters!"

This had all the boys laughing, with Javick blushing.

"You are amazing, Arinna Cabal," Cather leaned in to wipe sweat from the redhead's forehead. The dark-haired woman sat back against a pell and Arinna rested her head on the Shoutte sibling's shoulder. "I learned more in this class than all my war-master's lessons."

"My father is a great teacher," Arinna said quietly. "As are many of the teachers at the Academy. All I know, he and the other masters at the academy taught me." She laughed softly. "And I might have picked up a few tricks in some taverns here and there when I had some difference of opinions with ruffians."

"But it is more than just repeating lessons you learned, Arinna. You see things, were able to see each of our flaws, analyze them and help correct them; Zondra has touched you with their hand. Like my brother, so different in a way, yet …"

"Zondra?" Arinna said. "I thought that was the patron of healing?"

"Yes," Turar had his arm around his partner Thorvin, gently ruffling his hair. "But they are the dual nature of warrior and healer; I saw last night you also helped our kinsman after the battle. Surely the hand of Zondra was there of certain."

"My father is a healer as well," Arinna said. "He earned the king's honor in the Confederacy Wars for his healing. He believes that a warrior should know the body."

"You certainly do." Cather snickered, and it was Arinna's turn to blush.

"About me being only interested in fighting and eating," the redhead said. "Suppose we…"

"Dame Cather!" A breathless young clansman came running from the kitchens. "Come quickly, there is trouble at The Eye of Zondra!"

The five in the training yard could hear the terror in the young boy's voice and Arinna raced past him to run down the corridors to the dungeon stairs. Cather was not far behind on the stone steps into the depths.

They ran past the cells to the narrow stairs that lead into the cavern where The Eye of Zondra was located.

When they arrived at the bottom of the rough-hewn stairs, they were halted by two of the under-priests who held them back with staves.

"No, kinsfolk," the cleric said, "it is not safe to go any further."

Arinna ignored the religio, dodging under the staff barrier to round the corner to the vault door, there she stopped and gasped. The large brass-studded door with the symbol of Zondra on it was still closed, the steel bar still across it, but the bar was bowing out, the door itself distorted behind it.

The redhead could feel a deep chill coming from the warping door even across the open space. The strangeness of it halted her and she looked back at the under-priests.

"What is happening?"

"We do not know, dame," an acolyte guard said, as he knelt near the vault door, trying to comfort one of the other guards who was shivering and moaning. The under-priest in pain was cradling a right hand that looked burnt and blistered. "He tried to remove the bar when we heard the noise and saw the color change in the door."

Arinna heard it now, a low keening sound that climbed up and down the scale and seemed to leak out from the vault door. She took a halting step toward the door but as her hand came near the metal bar, the chill struck her in a hard wave of cold and she jumped back.

"Don't, dame!" the under-priest called.

"We have to do something!" the redhead said in frustration.

"Use this!" An out-of-breath Javick came charging in and held out one of the pot-holders he had run back to the kitchen to get. "Thorvin is bringing some of the meat hooks, but had to pull the svor haunches off them."

Arinna took the offered cloth and grabbed the bar, the horrid cold leaching through the rag into her hands but she gripped harder and worked

"...IT IS NOT SAFE TO GO ANY FURTHER..."

to pull the bar off. In a moment Thorvin raced up. He and Javick hooked the heavy metal hooks under the bar and the three of them pulled up. For a long moment, the cold and the distortion of the door were winning and then the bar jerked free and came up off its holdings.

The steel bar clattered to the ground and shattered when it hit the stone.

All three who had touched the bar were stunned by the cold that had traveled to their hands, Arinna cursing violently and shaking her hands to get blood back into her fingers.

"We have to try to pry the door open," she said. Her normally calm voice

Cather took a staff from one of under-priests and moved to the door, wedging the Ovar wood of it into an open space between the door and the surrounding frame. Turar joined her and the two worked to lever the door open until the staff snapped in half from the strain.

"No, by Zondra, no!" Cather cried. "Get to my brother!" As she spoke, the keening sound from the vault rose to a painful level that hurt their ears, driving them all to their knees with hands over ears to try and block the sound—then suddenly stopped as the door flew open.

The bent, twisted figure that appeared there, backlit by an eerie blue light, caused all those in the open space to gasp.

"Bukram's belt," Arinna cursed. "What happened?"

CHAPTER NINETEEN:
RESURRECTION

No one moved in the open stone space until the figure in the doorway shambled forward, a deep gasping sound issuing from it. "By the Rythem," the whispered words came out of the form as it pitched forward and fell headlong.

"Erique!" Arinna screamed and ran to her fallen friend, quickly joined by his sister.

The fallen clerical student was a hideous sight in the low light glowgems of the space. His pallor was chalky white, his eyes deep-set in their sockets and the skin on his cheeks drawn tight. He stared up at the others, having trouble focusing his eyes. He tried to speak but his throat was too tight and he was barely able to whisper.

"Death. Atrum," he managed. "Murder. Shadowcraft."

"Easy, brother," Cather said. "Rest, we will get Leanna."

Arinna was in tears as she cradled her friend's head in her lap. "What happened?"

"Darkness," he gasped. "D-d-darkness." Then he shivered and lapsed into unconsciousness.

The three sword student clansmen helped carry the unconscious Erique up the stairs but before she went up with them Arinna drew her rapier and stepped into The Eye of Zondra.

"By Yulin's Heart," she murmured. Cather and one of the under-priests joined her and what they saw drew more gasps from them. The whole shape of the interior of the room had been altered and now glowed blue. The crystal structure was clearly different with the very angle of the crystals changed and some of them even cracked and shattered.

"My kinsfolk," Cather whispered in horror when she saw the previous Shoutte's scattered around the room in their final resting places.

The bodies of Atrum and the others they could see clearly in the odd light were different now as well. The skin of each of the bodies was no longer the image of what they had been in life, but now looked more like waxy effigies of themselves, tinted blue-green by the crystal illumination.

On the floor at the center of the room was a black, dusty powder, arrayed in a wide circle around a single point. From that point emanated the stink of decay and death.

"This is unholy," Cather said, making the sign of Zondra in defense.

"Yes," Arinna said with a fierceness that scared her companion. "And it didn't happen by accident; your clan is most certainly under attack from within." The redhead moved forward to kneel in the center of the circle where there was a single black sphere that looked to be a flat-black stone. She poked it wit h her sword and when it did not react picked it up and examined it closely.

"The smell comes from this. But it seems safe enough." She placed it in her belt pouch and joined the Shoutte girl at the entrance to the vault.

"Seal this door," Cather ordered the clan members who had come down the stairs, attracted by the commotion. "And send Priest Ozam to The Shoutte's room; there must be cleansing rituals performed."

The two women raced up after the others and headed straight to Erique's suite.

"What in Zondra's name has happened to my brother?" Cather asked in horror as the two ran up the stairs.

"I swear we will find out, Cather," Arinna promised. "And when we do, someone will pay."

When they reached the bedroom of the suite where the desiccated man had been put to bed, the healer Leanna was already there by his side. In the clear light of the room his condition was even more shocking. His leg and shoulder wounds had opened again. Lying naked on the top of the covers while Leanna worked to clean the wounds, it was clear he had also, somehow, lost weight.

"Oh, my brother!" Cather cried. "Zondra preserve you."

At his sister's voice, Erique opened his eyes and looked at her and Arinna. He tried for a weak smile but it looked more like a rictus grin. He moved his lips but only the faintest whisper escaped him.

"The darkness," he said. "It was there; it reached for me."

"Easy, Erique," Arinna said, tears coming unbidden. "We will guard you. Nothing will get in here. Nothing, I swear on my mother." She held up the black sphere.

"No need," he smiled weakly. "It is gone back to the beginning of time, before all things. From whence it came. It was a thing from before even the age of wizards. It reached into my very soul. Or at least it tried to."

"We will find a way to fight it, to make you better," Cather said. "We will…"

"No. It is gone back to the darkness that it came from," he insisted. "You only hold the seed and skeleton of it."

"That mess on the floor of the vault?" Arinna asked.

He did manage a smile this time that was less hideous. "Yes, I was able to sing it back to its before time."

"It was the same thing that killed your brother, wasn't it?" Arinna surmised.

"Yes, just so," Erique raised his head to look Cather in the eyes. "He did not have the Kova to fight it with, I was blessed to have the Way in my heart; it was all I could do." The effort to speak drained him even more and his voice was barely a whispered croak. "It was a wave of a void, an emptiness at the core of reality. An unchanging nothingness that is the enemy of the Kova. It could not stand the light of The Way." He fell back to the pillow, his eyes closed, and sighed deeply. "I wish I could have been here for Atrum. He must have felt so alone."

Cather looked with confusion at Arinna, who was drying her tears.

"In his religion, the Kova says that change is everything, the center of all things," Arinna explained. "This thing that he describes would be the exact opposite of the Kova."

"Blasphemy," Ozam said from where he stood in the doorway to the room with Kurvan, having heard the last few exchanges. He made the sign of Zondra and waved an incense brazier to send wisps of smoke to dance around the room.

"There is no time for religion now," Cather rose to face the old man. "He is worse than I thought and needs to rest now."

"But to speak of such things," the priest said. "It is the vileness of the water goddess, from the old times." He made the sign of Zondra and hissed out the word, "Ashun" as a curse.

"Your clan leader just defeated the thing that killed your previous clan head," Arinna said, rising to full fury so that those in the room thought she might charge like a wild beast. "You can debate the finer points of religion later; but considering it was he who saved your miserable life last night you need to leave him time to heal. It was in The Eye of Zondra that he fought and defeated this abomination, so do you think Zondra was not on his side? Pray for him to Zondra and I will pray to him for Yulin. He will need all the gods and goddesses he we can summon to save him. Now let him rest."

"Parley," Erique abruptly whispered, interrupting all in the room. He pushed himself up on his side and fixed those in the room with his stare, his eyes bright with effort. "I must meet with the other clans to stop more attacks."

"But Erique—" Kurvan began.

"He needs quiet and food and rest," Leanna proclaimed with a sharp tone. "This mighty little one speaks truth; The Shoutte has proven himself enough twice over to all now and it must be by Zondra's hand that he lives. It could not be any other way. To say anything else is the blasphemy here. Now go!"

Everyone in the room felt the energy of her annoyance. Arinna stepped by the bed and knelt to put a hand on the wounded cleric's forehead.

"We'll take care of it, Erique," she said quietly. "Just rest."

Ozam began to say something but Kurvan waved him to silence. "You are right, of course, Auntie Leanna," Kurvan said before anyone could speak again. "He has sat a vigil such as no other Shoutte has endured but he did sit the vigil, all accept that. He came through to us in what is surely Zondra's mercy. He is indisputably The Shoutte. He is now in Leanna's hands." He turned to her with slight smile on his lips. "How may we help him best, kinwoman?"

"Send up hot broth and wine," Leanna said, curtly.

Kurvan waved the others to leave and they all moved to the outer chamber, leaving the old healer, Leanna, alone with Erique.

"Thank you, Lord Kurvan," Arinna said. "I will stay here with my friend, if you have no objection."

"Of course, dame. I will also have food sent up for you as well."

Turar headed to the door. "Let me bring the food," he raced off before any one could stop him.

"I will see that the riders go out to the clans as he directed," Kurvan said to Cather when she looked at him with searching eyes. "Who will see to the wounded below?"

"Leanna can, as soon as she has brother settled in, kinsman." She looked back to Arinna who smiled. "Dame Arinna will stay with Erique to keep guard."

The other two sword students looked to Cather and Arinna. "We would stay as well if we can be of service, Dame kinswoman," Jarvick said. Cather and Arinna both acknowledged the gesture with nods.

"Good," Kurvan said. "But we must keep this between us all and not let it be known how badly The Shoutte has been injured. It will shake the clan."

"He will be up and ready to fight quickly," Arinna said. The others looked at her with incredulous expressions. "I have seen him stabbed and bleeding and still able to take on two tavern thugs. Once he was sick with Carkon lung and still he rode two days to bring serum to a stricken village. He will be up soon." There was a desperate undercurrent to her voice that all in the room heard. No one dared contradict her.

Kurvan waved to Ozam. "Come, priest, we will do what must be done."

"I must go below to re-sanctify The Eye of Zondra," the old priest said. "And I will pray for The Shoutte." He gave a last look to Arinna as if he wanted to speak but chose to simply bless her with the Sign of Zondra.

Leanna came to the door from the inner chamber. "I heard, kinsfolk. I agree that Dame Arinna is best to keep watch on our Lord; I saw her last night she has skill as well. My patients below need me more. The Shoutte needs mostly rest; all else is in Zondra's hands and his own stubborn nature." She gave a little giggle. "Like his father and all the Shoutte men it is his greatest power."

"I will be back up as soon as I can," Cather said to Arinna in a soft tone. "I will see that the security of the hold stays at full wariness and send outriders to the nearby farmsteads to alert them there could be more to this; and I will send up Erique's healer's bag and some extra food for you."

Arinna managed a smile for Cather, then went back into the inner chamber to sit beside Erique's bed.

CHAPTER TWENTY:
PURPOSE

When Turar brought the broth for the sleeping Erique, and some food and wine for her to eat, Arinna closed the door to the sleeping chamber and sat alone with her friend.

In the dim glowgem light Erique's color was a little better than it had been in The Eye of Zondra chamber, but not by much. His even breathing, at least, gave her some comfort.

Arinna did not disturb him from the healing sleep to feed him, so set the soup near the room's small fire to keep it warm. She sipped some of the wine but had no appetite for the food. She simply sat and watched the gentle rise and fall of his chest. His breathing was shallow, but steady enough to keep her from tears.

She looked at the double brand on his chest, remembering that chest before the skill marks, when he was the young, skinny boy she first met in the training yard at the Academy. He was shy and would barely speak for fear his stutter would bring ridicule. It seemed a lifetime ago, and for her it almost was. She had been only nine and he was so tall and gangly, yet he never, from the first, regarded her smallness as making her feel less.

He had, in fact, taken her side when some of the other students had objected to her being in with older students because she was the head instructor's daughter. And she and Erique had shared secrets and friendships, hardships, fought back-to-back in barracks combats and become family. He had been there when her mother passed away from a sickness her father could not fight. It was Erique who held her while she cried through the night and had been the first to help her learn to laugh again and find joy again, even with recalling her mother with warmth instead of pain.

Erique moved in his sleep and made a deep sigh that was almost a moan.

"I told them you would recover completely, Erique," she whispered. "So you better. Don't make a liar of me."

The clerical student rolled on the bed and faced her, his eyes opening slightly. "No one can make you do anything you don't want to, Arinna," he whispered.

"How are you feeling?" she asked, working hard to smile for his sake.

"Like your father has made me do hard duty against the beginner students."

"Could you handle some broth?"

He nodded and she brought him some and ladled it out for him to sip. After a few minutes, he was able to sit up a little with her help and managed to sip from the bowl she held for him.

"Your sister and Kurvan are gathering the riders to send out and have seen to it that Stormrest is secure," Arinna said after a time. "Leanna is down stairs with the patients and is doing fine with them."

"Good." His voice was hoarse but stronger than it had been. "The riders must go out. We can not be seen to be weak; but we must act in some way, at least be seen to act."

There was a gentle knock on the door and Cather's voice asked, "Arinna?"

The redhead let the Shoutte girl in and rebarred the door.

"Brother." Cather stepped up to the bed and crouched to take Erique's hand. "We were so worried."

"You should have faith in Zondra," he said with a faint smile. "They would not desert Clan Shoutte."

Cather looked to Arinna then back to him. "I thought you did not believe in Zondra anymore?"

"That is the mistake so many make about the Kova," he said. "We accept all gods but simply believe that the principle of eternal change is supreme to all. Everything changes, that is the cycle of the world. Life and death, winter to summer; that is the Kova. So all are in harmony with that principle, regardless of the religion."

Cather took this in with a quizzical expression but after a time asked, "What happened in The Eye of Zondra? Was what killed Atrum the same thing that almost killed you?"

He took another sip of broth from the bowl as Arinna held it for him. After a few moments he looked at his sister again and said, "All life is vibration; each of us is a song the universe sings. This thing I encountered was a song sung in discord to living things and I reached into my soul and greeted it with the song of life and harmony. It was exactly opposite its evil reality."

Cather looked puzzled, but Arinna said, "The priests of the Kova can sing to speed healing, to even make plants grow faster. I have seen it."

"But there is also War Voice," Erique said, "that can cause death. I thought it a legend before this, but now I know it must have been real, for this thing I encountered in the vault was the embodiment of the song of death; a thing called up from the very beginnings of all things, from before time itself."

Arinna reached over to hug Cather as she shivered at his statement. "Where did it come from?"

"I can not say but I am sure it could not have been in the vault naturally. As it was not in this suite naturally when it took our brother from us."

"A traitor?" Cather paled.

"What other answer? With the postern gate opened and with me deliberately targeted in the attack in the hall as well?"

"Yet you would ride to Parley with the clans?" The dark-haired girl looked at Arinna as if to get her to talk Erique out of his intent, but the redhead just shrugged.

"Yes," he managed. "The sooner I can bring this to the other clans the better; there is some dark force at work here and all of Umbria could be in danger."

"You can't ride anywhere," Cather argued. "You can not even stand, brother, let alone ride the many miles to the Parley circle. The trip alone would kill you."

"No, I can not ride yet," he said with a ghost of a smile flitting across his face, "but soon I will."

"Not soon. You look like I feel after Master Rhemlly's Old Kingdom wrestling class," Arinna said, "only worse."

"I have to, Arinna," he said grimly. "Shoutte can not stand alone against this kind of darkness; especially if there is someone in the hold connected to those bandits who attacked us. The strength of Shoutte must be aligned with the strength of all the highlands."

"You will do no one any good if you kill yourself," Cather said.

"Do I have to fight both of you?"

They both said, "Yes!" at the same time, then looked at each other and giggled.

"I surrender," he conceded, "but only for now; but I pledge I will make the ride in a day or two."

"We will talk then," Cather said. "It will take that long until word comes from the clans in any case."

"Then I will sleep, sister. Please follow the protocol and set the meeting for the arches at Parley Circle."

"Yes, I will see to it that riders and ko'ta messages are sent out. Now, sleep. When you wake, we will see if Arinna has left any food in the kitchens for you."

"Hey," the redhead said.

The wounded clerical student smiled and closed his eyes. In a moment he was deep asleep.

Arinna and Cather moved quickly to the door, opened it and stepped outside into the office, but left the door open a crack to be able to keep an eye on Erique.

"He looks so feeble." Now that she did not have to keep up a heroic front, Arinna could let her fear of losing her friend leap to the surface and she sobbed, tears coursing down her cheeks. "He's lost weight, he … he … I've never seen him so close to death…"

"Easy," Cather hugged the smaller woman. "He is The Shoutte of Shoutte. He will find his strength, I am sure."

"I am not," Arinna admitted. "I have never seen him so … *so.*"

"No. You can not think that way. You were the one who told me to have faith in him at his contest. He will recover. Now he needs our faith more than ever. The question will be whether it is soon enough to matter with the Parley."

"And if Erique can not make the trip?"

"Then as next in line I will have to go as his emissary," Cather suggested. "And hope I can do as he would wish; I will ask him what his intent will be if it comes to that."

"How long till the trip must happen?"

"If the other clans agree it will be perhaps three days or four at the most."

"By then—," Arinna looked up with a wan smile and new courage. "By then he'll be ready to teach sword class to all of us, I am sure."

CHAPTER TWENTY-ONE:
THE SHOUTTE COMMANDS

In fact, it was two days before Erique could stand to walk, but by the end of the first day he was already taking interest in clan affairs, though he had to take frequent naps to renew himself. Kurvan visited several times to report that he had seen to all the guards, both in the hold and outriders as well, and provided details of information that had come in from svorherders that thefts were indeed up again.

Cather was in and out all day to check up on her brother's progress, though he slept more than he was awake, and to visit Arinna, who set up a sleeping pallet in the bedchamber so she could spend all her time with Erique should he need anything.

Turar, Thorvin and Javick stayed in the outer office and acted as an unofficial bodyguard to the new Shoutte of Shoutte. When she saw their devotion to her brother Cather relieved them of other clan duties and made their positions official by the end of the first day.

Arinna continued lessons for the three—and Cather when she could spare time—in the limited space of the outer office. They added dagger fighting to their curriculum and some wrestling and they were constantly surprised at the depths of her combat knowledge and insight to flaws and strengths.

By the end of the first day Erique was able to sit up and watch through the open door and make comments,. The others found the exchanges between Arinna and the new Lord a constant source of amusement as they fenced almost as much with their jibes as anyone else did with swords.

By the second evening Erique was eating almost as much as Arinna—between naps.

Many of those that had come for the vigil and funeral had left the hold, returning to their farmsteads but with an understanding that they could be called to arms at any moment to defend the clan and with a warning to stay extra vigilant for enemies.

"You will not be able to ride to Parley Circle tomorrow, brother," Cather said, when she sat to evening meal. Erique, Arinna and the three sword students were seated around the table that had been brought into the outer office along with sleeping pallets for the three new clan bodyguards.

"Why not?" Erique's color had returned and his tone was steady though his voice still a little hoarse. He washed down avrum steak with ale, with as much vigor as any of the others.

"You can't fool me," Cather said. "I saw you walk out here before; you had trouble doing that. If you can not walk across a room, how can you ride for a day and a half travel to the Parley Circle? Let alone stand tall to represent Shoutte?"

"Because I have to. If the word comes back that the clans will meet, they will accept no one but The Shoutte to the meeting."

"The word did come back an hour ago," Cather said. "The Sween and Ranor have agreed, as have a few of the smaller unaffiliated clans. We have not heard from the Kreill."

"They have to come if the others have agreed. They will have heard of it and be afraid not to come for fear they will be conspired against if they do not show up. In this case highland suspicions will work for us."

"But..." she started.

"It doesn't matter what you say, Cather, he will do it," Arinna said with a shake of her head. "I have seen that look in his eye before, too often. When he is convinced he is right, nothing will stop him."

"But he is in no condition to make the ride and no wagon can make it over that trail." Cather looked to the three clansmen for support but they looked to Arinna.

Arinna smiled. "I don't think any of us could stop him, even in the shape he is in, but don't worry, he will not be riding alone."

"Wait a minute," Erique said. "I have to go to Parley as a leader, alone. You know, Cather, that the clans only respect strength and this must be a meeting of clan heads only."

"We will ride with you to just out of sight," Arinna clarified. "Just in case; you will get to ride in alone."

"That will be difficult," Cather said. "The Parley Circle is west of here, on what used to be an island in the center of a lake; years ago an earthquake caused the lake to drain, leaving the island as a high point. It sits above the wide plain surrounding it. Anyone riding to the island is visible for half a day; that is why it is still the neutral ground here in Umbria. It is at the extreme edge of the Shoutte lands but reachable by the other clans without having to venture too far into any other clan's lands to be at risk."

"So, we ride to the border of the plain with Erique, then hold back in

"THAT WILL BE DIFFICULT," CATHER SAID.

case he needs us on this island," Arinna said. "If he does, we ride fast." She spoke as if there was no other answer. Cather shot her a look to disagree but the redhead simply took a sip of ale and smiled.

Thorvin, the broadest of the three sword students, who was also the most musical, smiled and sang a ditty he had composed earlier while they practiced. "*The redhead charged, her sword held high and giggled as she did, and all who had opposed her, ran away and hid!*"

Everyone at the table laughed, Erique so hard that he had to grab the wound on his hip.

+++

The morning of the fourth day after his vigil in The Eye of Zondra, the new Shoutte of Shoutte ordered that his mount be saddled and prepared to head to the Parley Circle.

Kurvan, Cather, Leanna and several others objected but their protests were pushed aside.

Arinna and her three students also obtained mounts and a good supply of food were waiting patiently in the courtyard of Stormrest while Erique spoke with Kurvan and Cather.

"I think your actions are wrong for the clan, Erique," the older Shoutte protested. "Even if you were not clearly weakened, which will reflect badly on the clan, you are playing into the hands of whomever attacked us by begging for help from the others."

"I will not be begging. And my physical state matters less than my resolution to solve this problem. Real strength comes from within, good uncle. If they will not join to a collation they will have doomed themselves, I am sure."

"I agree with Kurvan that it appears to be that Shoutte is begging for help," Cather had stopped trying to convince her brother that he could not make the trip in his weakened state.

"It is not begging to unite," Erique rebutted. "It was not begging when our grandfather, The Shoutte, asked the clans to unite against the Mephan incursion three generations ago."

"That was different," Kurvan insisted. "This is a Shoutte matter."

"No, it isn't," Erique argued. "We were attacked by outlaws, our herds raided. I am sure many other clans are in the same situation. Atrum and I were attacked by Shadowcraft, and I have no doubt all these events are linked. I am sure the other clans are equally at risk."

"You do not know this for sure," Kurvan said.

"How sure do we have to be?" Erique countered as he moved haltingly to mount his vorn. "More certain than the blood of two score kin? No. The other clans will have had the same problems, I am sure of it. If they had not, they would not have agreed to Parley."

"At least let me ride with you, brother."

"No," he wheeled his mount around and pointed for the gate. "If you are right, dear sister and I am wrong then after I am dead you will have to lead the clan to avenge me as the next Shoutte."

There was nothing that could be said to argue with that so, with no further discussion he rode out at an easy gait with the three clansmen and Arinna, cursing her vorn already, keeping pace.

+++

"You should not be in the saddle," Arinna said when the group had been on the road for only a few hours, heading cross-country toward the Parley Circle. "You look worse than I usually do on vornback."

Erique, slumped over the pommel when they stopped to water the vorns, looked at Arinna with hooded, hollow eyes. "I have to confess I am having trouble staying awake. I feel so weak."

"I hate to agree with what Cather said back at Stormrest. But I am beginning to think you are not going to be up to this meeting."

"No," Erique said with forced energy. "I have to be the one or all the clans will think Clan Shoutte weak."

"You will do nothing for the clan if you fall off your vorn and break your neck because you can't stay awake."

"If I may," Turar interrupted. "The Parley Circle is easily a full day ahead. I am sure Lord Shoutte will be fine if he could rest for another day."

"How are we going to let him rest and still get there?" Thorvin asked. "Suddenly discover a warp portal?"

"No," Turar shot back to his lover with an angry glare. "But on the farmstead I grew up on, I have seen mothers who take their newborns with them when plowing by setting a sling between the two harnessed plow vorns. The action of the two animals walking in unison lulls the child to sleep."

Arinna laughed. "That is the best idea I have ever heard in my entire life."

"No," Erique tried and failed to muster the energy for a strong objection as he was having trouble staying upright in the saddle.

In short order the others had harnessed two of the vorns side by side with a blanket slung between then into a hammock for the complaining lord of the clan. Arinna laughed almost constantly during the process.

And so, Erique, the new Shoutte of Shoutte rode to Parley sleeping most of the trip, strapped between two vorn in a hammock, like a newborn, in hopes of regaining the strength he knew he would need to save his clan from extinction.

CHAPTER TWENTY-TWO:
PARLEY

"You are doing this just to get back at me," Arinna said from her hiding place in a sack slung on the side of a pack.

"I would never do that," he said with a sly grin as their two vorns approached the base of the Parley Circle escarpment. It was clear that it had been an island by the steep upsweep of the sides. "That would be a vindictive act and I am above such things."

"I will make you pay for this," she hissed. "At least tell me where we are."

"Almost at the base of the island right where the stone steps are. I can see the vorns of the other clans tied up ahead of us."

"Is there anyone around?"

"Not that I can see. Once we get to the base and I am sure we are alone, you will be able to come out."

"I still don't see why I couldn't just ride up with you."

"Because I can explain you away as a neutral outsider in person, but from a distance you could be mistaken for a clan warrior in violation of the tenets."

"But I'm not neutral."

"You and I both know that." He dismounted and tied his mount's reins to a wooden hitching post. "But when they see you have no clan mark, they may believe it." He stretched to relieve a cramp, feeling much refreshed from his day-long doze, but still sore and more tired than he wanted to admit. He grabbed a wine skin and took a long swig then walked around for a few minutes, looking at the squirming sack containing his friend and smiling.

He located the food preparation area near the steps that lead up into the Parley Circle itself, as not even knives were allowed up top, an outdoor kitchen with knives and cooking implements were maintained. Though they could cook on the circle anyone they would cut and prepare it off island.

Can I really do this? He asked himself. *Was Cather right? Have I brought my clan to a terrible place?*

After a time Arinna called from the sack. "Why have we been stopped for so long?"

"I was scouting to be sure we are alone." Erique backed away from the vorn, suppressing outright laughter. "We are here, you can come out."

There was a moment when there was no movement, then a moan as the red-haired girl burst from the sack and promptly fell face forward to the ground.

"Bukrum's belt!" she cursed as her face landed in the dirt.

Erique worked manfully to suppress laughing. "The oddest birth I have ever seen!"

"My legs are asleep," she tried to stand. She looked up at him and made a face. "You could help me, you know?"

"I could, but this is too entertaining to watch."

"When I can stand you had better be able to run."

It took her several minutes to get full circulation and Erique used the time to unpack some preserved meats and wine skins. When she approached him, he held up some svor jerky as a peace offering to her.

"So, I can't even bring a dagger?" She accepted the food and a swig of wine to wash it down.

"No weapons on Parley Circle island. I am pushing the limits of what I may be allowed by bringing you as an advisor- there is some precedent for it in the records. I am afraid, Arinna, you were right, I am not powerful enough to face this alone and as much as I don't like to admit it, I do draw strength from you."

She swallowed the food quickly and put a hand on her friend's arm. "You said the others will only respect strength and as much as I want to be there, I have been reconsidering that. I can't think it makes you look very strong to bring me."

He smiled. "Well, they don't know you like I do so they will not realize you are a formidable warrior. They will view you as simply a helper."

"Helper?"

"And advisor. Do not be upset," he laughed, "but honestly, I have to act strong and sure in front of the others of the clan, but not with you. I do not know if this is the right thing to do, or if I am up to it, but I do know that once I am up on that island what I do will affect the lives of everyone in my clan. And the other clans. Your counsel keeps me from believing my own lies and you see things tactically with even statements as much as with weapons." His strength and vitality seemed to leave him and his shoulders sagged. "I was able to appear certain this far, but I just…"

"Stop it, Erique, now is not the time to doubt yourself. You know I couldn't do what you have done and I still don't know how you stay calm all the time. I can't think of all the times you've kept me from making a mistake or two or three in a single day. How could I not be here for you?"

"I knew you wouldn't fail me," he smiled. "You may be the one thing in this world that the Kova does not apply to—you are unchanging."

"Let's get up that trail, then. I hope they have hot food."

"Okay, helper. I'd better go first; I wouldn't want the sight of you to scare them."

✦✦✦

The top of the island was a rocky plateau with low scrub brush in vivid blues and reds. It sloped slightly toward the center where the land rose to a central hill. On that hill were ruins of an old temple to the ancient, banned religion, the worship of Ashun, that had been reconsecrated to Zondra just before the earthquake that drained the lake.

There was a small fire burning in a pit, surrounded by simple wooden benches set amidst the fallen columns. All was beneath two stone arches that still stood as the ruins of the temple. Not far from it was a simple shack where a guardian of Zondra, priest or priestess lived year-round by the charity of the clans to function as a mediating figure for any inter-clan disputes, though in the last few years it was a little used tradition. The guardian changed yearly and the current priestess was near the end of her year-long term.

Several figures stood around the leaping flames of the fire. All heads turned to look at Erique and Arinna as the two friends emerged from the slightly sunken path from the island's base.

Seven stood there, six in clan kilts and one, older woman wearing the robes of a priestess of Zondra.

"I see Sween, Ranor, Kreill, Xon and Scall patterns," Erique whispered to Arinna, pointing out each design for the clans. "And that black kilt is from the unaffiliated coalitions."

"They don't look very cheerful," the redhead whispered as the two friends crossed the open space and moved through the ruins to what had once been the central room of an old building. They kept their hands away from their body, palms outward to it was clear they had no weapons on them.

"Who comes before the council of clans?" the old priestess asked in formal tones as she surveyed them, a little confused as she looked at the red haired girl who was with the tall highlander.

"I am The Shoutte of Shoutte."

"You wear no clan mark," the priestess stepped forward and peered at the clerical student, raising her eyebrows when she saw the brand on Erique's chest. "And you have this strange mark."

"He is the young one who has been out-country," a grey-bearded, shaven-headed man who wore the clan mark of the Ranor said. "I have heard tales of him." He looked directly at Arinna when he spoke again and the insult was clear. "And what is this?"

The redhead stiffened but kept her smile fixed and her physical attitude looking relaxed.

"Easy, Arinna," Erique whispered as he looked directly into the bearded man's eyes.

"This, good Ranor, is Dame Arinna Cabal. She is not of Umbria and so not obligated to any clan here as my advisor and has some special knowledge that may be of use to this council."

There was a long pause while all the others looked at each other as if to see if anyone would object.

The grey-haired Ranor took up the implied challenge from the others. "Seems to me that what he have here are two whelps, too young to decide for any clan."

Erique stepped forward and squatted by the fire to make a show of warming his hands. He worked to not show how his hip bothered him with the action and looked up to smile with apparent genuine joy at the man who had spoken. "Well, good father Ranor, since our ages added together do not nearly equal yours, we will listen to your good counsel with the enthusiasm of youth after we have informed you why I, as Shoutte of Shoutte called this most vital Parley."

"All the highland clans and their allies are now represented here," the priestess said, still speaking with a formal and neutral. She stepped in to stop any more conversation, raising her blessing stick to wave it over the fire. "It is as it was in the day of the Great Coalition against the accursed Mephan invaders; then it was that The Shoutte called rival clans to stand with him for the greater good of all the highlands against those and all outsiders. Then the blessings of Zondra allowed for victory. We call on Zondra now to bless this gathering that all may speak only truth."

The priestess stepped back and all but Arinna gave the sign of Zondra in answer to the priestess's symbol. It consisted of both hands touching the center of the chest, crossed over each other in an X shape then opening out palm up.

Arinna made the blessing sign of Yulin, touching her heart with the edge of her right hand in a fist the opened the palm, meaning she was open to the Goddess.

The older priestess's voice rang out. "All stand and declare that you bring no weapon and speak only the truth under penalty of Zondra's eternal punishment!"

"I, Erique of Shoutte so declare."

"I, Tandor of the Ranor so declare."

"I, Voran of the Sween so swear," a short-haired and sword-scarred woman, a decade older than Erique said. She had a broken nose and regarded the two new arrivals with predatory eyes.

The redhead returned Voran's stare with emerald sharp eyes. "I, Arinna of Cozen, with no clan affiliation so declare."

"I, Rolar, representing the unaffiliated 'steads, so swear." He, like Tandor had a shaved head but only had a full bushy mustache.

"I, Kort of the Scall so declare." He was a slight, older man, not tall, but his muscles were whipcord and his expression sour.

"I Dolit of the Xon so swear." He was the shortest of the group, but broad with long arms that seemed to reach almost to his knees.

All eyes turned to the last of those around the fire. She was the tallest one in the group, her long raven hair plaited to two braids. She was also more than a decade older than Erique and wore the firehawk design on her kilt. In addition to her clan tattoo on her left cheek she had a firehawk tattoo on her left shoulder and arm that wound around the limb.

She met the gaze of all the others one at a time, finally locking eyes with Erique. "I, Uta of the Kreill so declare."

There was a sudden collective exhale and a palpable sense of relief from all who stood around the fire pit.

"Then let us eat and drink, then speak convivially," the old priestess said in a slightly less formal tone. She seemed pleased to have the company.

"Now that is something I can do as good as any highlander," Arinna said quietly to Erique. "I'm starving."

CHAPTER TWENTY-THREE:
TREACHERY

The group around the fire ate stew and bread and drank wine from skins provided by the priestess, quietly regarding each other with suspicious eyes. Since not even knives were allowed on the parley ground, ceramic ladles were used to dish out the precut svor stew that had been prepared at the cooking station at the bottom of the Parley Circle steps, off the island.

The old priestess, Romark, gave a blessing as she handed out each bowl. She made long eye contact with Erique but said nothing more about the clearly visible brand on his chest.

After the smaller Younger Brother set, its Older Brother cast a purple haze over the whole of the raised island and lengthened the shadows. It gave the ruins an eerie cast and all the eyes of the participants were constantly assessing the other clans with suspicious glances.

After a time, when all had emptied their bowls and were waiting for the next development all eyes turned to look to Erique who spoke softly but with purpose.

"Clans folk, I called this most sacred Parley Circle because there is a very real threat to all the highlands."

"Because your brother died?" Dolit asked. "How exactly does that affect us?"

"Because he was murdered, Dolit; because the means of his death was a foul form of shadowcraft not seen here for millennium here in the highlands. Because my clan was attacked by an organized group of outlaws numbering over a hundred and the svor herds have been stripped in largest numbers ever. And because I believe all these events are connected and bode dark times for not just Clan Shoutte but for all of the clans of Umbria."

"I still do not see how this affects us," Tandor of the Ranor said. He refilled his wine tankard while leering at Arinna, all but ignoring Erique. "We are strong, we need no out-clan help."

"You know you have greater losses this season than last season," Erique countered. "And that they have increased each season for several." Arinna looked at him, arching an eyebrow, but he gestured subtly to quiet her.

"You know no such thing."

Erique smiled.

"And you, Uta," Erique continued, "the Kreill think it was the Xon or the Shoutte." When he saw shocked expressions of the other clan leaders, he knew that all of Cather's suspicions she had communicated to him were true. It only emboldened him to push on.

He looked around the circle into the eyes of each leader. "You all have experienced losses that you will not talk about for fear of giving advantage to the others or worse, appearing weak. You have had drover disappearances and other unexplained occurrences. Your nekot caravans have not been through the pass this year at all."

"You are just guessing," Uta said. She stood, apparently hoping her height would intimidate Erique. It did not. He stood to look up into her eyes while giving an easy smile. She was a full two inches taller than he.

"Only on some of it," he admitted, "but I know for a fact that no caravans have gotten through. And I do know that none of you would be here if you did not think there was something wrong with that attack on Shoutte. In other times you might even rejoice in it but these strange days, I think you are all a bit frightened by it."

"The Sween are frightened of nothing," Voran said, shooting to her feet.

"Nor are the Scall," Kort snarled.

"No?" Erique shot back. "Yet you are here."

"To face the accusations of a bare-faced, unmarked boy?" Tandar rose to stand beside Uta and Voran to face Erique. "A boy who abandoned the old ways for foreign religions."

"I have not abandoned Zondra or the heritage of my forbearers," Erique said. "That I am here before you should be proof enough of that. I sat the vigil. I am The Shoutte."

Arinna stayed seated but shifted her weight to the balls of her feet, ready to spring like a wild tvek. Erique noticed and shook his head subtly to dissuade her from action.

"No violence on this sacred place," Romark said. She too rose to step forward, extending her staff like a barrier in front of Erique.

"None will happen, good mother," Erique said calmly. "They know I speak the truth. It is just understandable that they just do not want to appear weak in front of each other."

"The Xon are not weak."

"No, you most definitely are not." Erique leaned on a fallen stone working to look casual, but Arinna could tell in the dancing firelight that he was doing it because he was suddenly tired. "None of us are weak, nor are any of you foolish enough to turn your eyes away from a danger to your peoples. Search your hearts and your minds; think about the losses from this past season. In the sight of Zondra can you deny these things have been happening? And if they are happening to you, realize they are happening to your neighbors as well."

The others looked back and forth waiting for each other to speak in the negative, but it was Uta who spoke first.

"If these things you say are true, what can be done, Shoutte?"

"We can ally guards on our herds. We can open the old watch towers from the Great Coalition days and be ready to help when an attack such as occurred at Shoutte befalls any one of the other of you, as I am sure will happen. For now whoever is behind the attack on Shoutte will be emboldened by the slaughter and I am sure fearful that this very meeting is a possibility."

"How can you be sure such a thing will happen again?" Kort asked.

"Because if you could attack any clan with impunity," Erique said, "or raid any herd or nekot caravan heading to the port with no consequences and had no ethics about it, wouldn't you take advantage of the divisions among us to do so?"

"If I were an outlaw band, yes, I would," Uta laughed. "You have a devious mind, Erique of Shoutte."

"Don't all us highland-bred folk," he said. This made several of the group grunted with humor.

"I can say that Sween herds were down this year," Voran looked shyly at the others. "And two farmsteads were raided two moons ago. Nine dead with no survivors and no idea who actually perpetrated the attack. There were none left behind of the raiders and no survivors of our clanskin."

"I did not hear of that," Tandor said with deep annoyance. "But I will admit that several of our herders have disappeared, along with two score or more of svor."

"You must have the sight," Rolar of the coalition said, as he stroked his mustache in a nervous gesture.

"No," Erique said. "Neither craft nor sight, but I know Umbrian clans would never act so dishonestly. If the Kreill or Sween wanted to destroy the Shoutte or any other clan you would face us in open combat; no one here would skulk like thieves. You all live in the light of Zondra. It is why even in far away Cozen I was proud to be a highlander of Umbria. It is why, when my clan needed me I returned."

"Zondra indeed blesses this gathering," Romark smiled at the group. "Let us sit again and consider the words of The Shoutte in these most serious matters."

"What else have you schemed, young Shoutte?" Uta asked in an almost jocular tone.

"Well," Erique looked from Uta to a still skeptical Tandor. "We are all hunters so we all know that if we can determine a prey's habits, divine their ways and trails, we can anticipate and trap or kill them. Find their dens and watering holes, see what patterns they have in their hunts and we know when and where is best to take them."

"So?" Tandor said.

"I think if we can gather all the dates and places of the thefts or attacks," Erique said. "We might be able to find a pattern to anticipate the next attacks, or at least backtrack them to wherever they come from or possibly to where they take the svor."

"It stands to reason they have to have somewhere to keep any stolen animals," Dolit said.

"And if, as you say, we all have had some thefts," Voran said grudgingly, "they have a considerable number of animals by now."

"And that would mean a number of people to watch those herds," Uta observed. "They would need a good number of brigands for that."

"And a system to keep them hidden; lookouts, some sort of food stores or what point to steal them to let them starve to death?" Tandar added, "These hills are full of canyons and blind valleys, but they would have to keep any decent-sized herd moving to keep from starving them or else the purpose to steal them would be pointless."

"Very much as I supposed might be so," Erique said. "I knew our combined minds would find a solution."

"You have thought this out well, Shoutte," Rolar said. "By bringing this to us you demonstrate a level head that shows Shoutte blood runs true from your grandfather."

"I thank you for that. I know from my dealings with the foreign world that many minds working on a problem are better than just one. And I knew, Rolar, that the clans would see the wisdom to unite when they realized the danger. These outlaws counted on the age-old divisions we all have had by keeping the attacks small enough to not raise the alarm, so the word would not spread far outside each hold's walls. They were hoping the natural competition between us would be our downfall. If there is any weakness in we of the highlands it is this suspicion between us."

"But why the attack on Shoutte?" Uta asked.

"Yes, that seems self-defeating if these brigands wanted to keep their activities secret," Dolit said.

"That I can not say," Erique confessed. "It has puzzled me as well—it seems that they might have been able to continue this pattern for a considerable more time. Perhaps my brother might have suspected something or learned something that led to his being murdered to stop him from revealing their plans. For that he was foully murdered!"

Arinna, who had remained silent but alert during all the discussion caught Erique's eye and, with a nod from him, spoke up now. "I know I have no formal voice here, but I think the fact that Erique came here with his outland ideas must have scared these bandits. They were rightly, it seems, afraid he would see what was really happening. He had been away long enough to notice the differences that those who live here might not for the gradual progression of things. He would see what was not right, not what was and that may have moved them into panicking."

"The little one is correct," Tandor said. "I am sure that none of us would have had the spleen to call this gathering or the distance from it all to see the problem."

Arinna did not even mind his comment, smiling at his conclusion.

Erique accepted the compliment and said, "I thank you for that, highlanders. Together I know we can stop this menace."

Everyone agreed and there was a tangible lessening of tension in the group as they sat and reached for the wine skin. The group discussed arrangements for exchanging representatives and information about the attacks and mutual assistance agreements. This discussion went on for several hours as the moons rose and set.

The old priestess, who was grinning like an expectant mother, brought out vellum and an inkwell and agreements were drawn up before the group finally agreed to sleep.

That was when the attack began!

END OF BOOK ONE:

A GLOSSARY OF ALTIVAN WORDS AND PHRASES

Altura: the name for the southern continent of Altiva.

Amarians: Dark skinned natives of Amaria on the southern continent.

Avrum: small furred flightless bird, a mammal (roughly shaped like a beaver) that burrows and is sought after for the meat.

Ashun: Water Goddess of the Mephan empire

Bot-Bot: a whiskered fish common in several varieties across the world.

Borakian Pirates: that ply the southern waters.

Carkon lung: a fungal lung infection

Clans of Umbria: Sween, Ranor, Kreill, Shoutte, Xon and Scall with un-affiliated clans wearing black kilts.

Clazbear: large mammal up to 12 feet tall with a single eye in the center of its forehead. Rare in the western portions of Ell'en .

Crystalscript: The Altiva equivalent of a money order—it is used across borders and honored by most of the different nations whose currency do not exchange well.

Darkhaven: town on the very southern continent.

Elder and Younger Brothers: the two suns of Altiva - The large blue Elder and smaller, 'faster' Younger is red.

Farport: Coastal town on the southern continent

Freshbowl: A crystalsmith creation that arrested any degeneration of organic material placed in it, effectively a stasis.

Gaddias ritual – advanced musical religious ceremony.

Goranga: ape/bear like beast who walks on two hooves and stands twice the height of a man. Red and brown speckled fur, though some rare ones can be white.

Gypher: large rodent like creature know to be both slow and stupid. Derogatory slang name for Valusian traveler race of Stavos

Iskarian Monk Style: A two-handed sword style also called "old Kingdom Style" that was used by the Mephan based Monks who followed Iskaria, the smiling pot bellied god who preaches peace and harmony but was also patron of warriors.

Joradorians: ancient cult on the southern continent mostly wiped out by the Mephans.

Juva Ale: potent beer ale made from the Juva berry which grows on bushes.

Julka Fruit: blue colored fruit that is sweet, like a passion apple.

Juasca: medicinal leaf for swelling reduction.

Khonal: The military sword dance of the Tolan Border Guard

Ko'ta: a bird common through much of Altiva's southern regions with unusual telepathic powers.

Kova nasta, kova kunda: *Strength of saints, strength of sinners* – Old Kovar language

Kukora: large, pterodactyl like birds.

kulva: Meaty bird raised for meat.

Linguaring: the Crystalsmith provided device that allows its wearer to understand any spoken language on Altiva.

Mephan: the island continent where the Mephan Empire originated. It was a large war-like nation that, for many generations ruled much of the world with an iron hand, using Shadow Craft and military force. As is the case with many empires it over extended their reach and then crumbled from within as many nations fought for and achieved their independence.

Mortag: Similar to thodist it can relieve muscle pain that way, but the raw leaf can be fatal. As a paste with a few things added it is safe and works for deep muscle relaxation.

Nikot: plant grown in Umbria and other mountainous regions that provides fibers like wool for clothing and which can also be eaten, often used for animal fodder.

Of the Shadows: term for a person who is two faced, specifically one who practices the shadowcraft or sorcery. Can also refer to a simple 'two face' person or liar.

Ovarwood: the wood that, my universal law, all doors to Inn's and Taverns *must* be made. A rare wood, extremely hard and can only be purchased from a Crystalsmith's Guild member.

Poisons: *Thoan, Thodist or Dillish Weed, Corvalish—Thodist and Dillish weed can be used for medicine.*

Priest-Voice: The unique vocal ability of the Kovar Order to send out several frequencies of sounds so that they could affect organics or living tissue to cause positive cellular activity to speed healing, plant growth and even increase the effectiveness of medicines.

Shadow Craft: the Altiva term for dark arts (in a world with two suns anything with one shadows is considered untrustworthy.

Skunda: lake serpent-like fish.

Svor: a slow, large lizard herd animal raised for meat and milk

Sweetcup: a crystal vessel to make any wine or ale literally taste sweeter.

Tall Grass: like bamboo.

Tvek: a pack animal. A reptile-like creature with a beak who is known for its savagery but can be domesticated if raised from an early enough age.

The Twin Sisters: the two moons of Altiva

The Rythem: the supreme principle of the Kova religion that holds that change is the only constant in the universe. (also written in the older text as Rhythem)

uvan dosta: the healing chants of Saint Scoran

Vindras Di: song cycle of the Yulin religion.

Vinta grass: a type of forage for animals…

Vorn: the beaked riding animal of Altiva. Some have antlers and all split hooves.

Warp Portals: an everyday part of Altivan life. Some occur naturally but most are created by warp wizards.

The warps are the remnants of a civilization so old its name had been lost in the mists of history. Only the warp wizards and their sometime allies, the crystalsmiths, still retained any of the old knowledge of that technology. Of these two classes the crystalsmiths came most in contact with the common folk. The wizards however were almost a race apart aloof from the cares of the populace.

Younger Brother (smaller blue sun) //Elder Brother larger red sun.

Yulin: The Goddess of Mercy and wisdom

Zamar: a red leafed bush.

Zondra: the Dual God: the chief religion of the Umbrian nation, Highland and low— two personalities in one, warrior and healer.

zor: Mephan currency (equal to 1 +3/4 Tollars (Tolan//Cozen currency).

'Z'n klar, keith nort yon'": <The people of the heart are of the blood.> Z'n Language

Z'n s'a: an island of off the west coast of the northern continent that means "Home of the people."

The Religions of Altiva:

Kova: (people the Kovar) Not a god/goddess but a principle of eternal change. Symbol the Omphast.

Svora: an off shoot religion of the Kova that have marriage for life, and are more into individual idols – their version of the Omphast is three squares as opposed to the Three Diamonds of the Kovar.

Zondra: Duel God/Goddess of the Umbrian Highlands

Ashun: Water Goddess of ancient origin—her cult was a destructive one women centric and murderous—snuffed out in the northern continent but stil active in the south.

Yulin: Goddess of hope and fertility

Mazdor: Victish god of creation- 'The Hungry One"

The Triad:

Gods worshiped by the Assassin's Guild.

Lukaz: god of just vengeance,

Shirra: the goddess of the slain

Iskaria: the smiling pot bellied monk god who preaches peace and harmony but was also patron of warriors.

The Five:

The Five, animal and human shapes joined in various awe inspiring forms that were the official religion of the country A Valdesta, Markoffanism

These are the slightly different versions of the Triad with the addition of the last two

Lukaz: god of just vengeance,

Shirra: the goddess of the slain

Iskari: the smiling pot bellied monk god who preaches peace and harmony but was also patron of warriors.

Makari: trickster Goddess,

Vuton: tvek-headed thief god of fertility

Markoffanism: The prophet Markoffan founded this religion, which, while it worships The Five is a repressive and radical religion which has no respect for women (in fact some sect cut the tongues out of women since their voices have no value)

THE TARROW OF ALTIVA.

The origins of the Tarrow Cubes are lost in time but they are thought to have come from the Yoni Stones (three carved stones used for divination in the old, Yoni religion) since the word Tarrow translates as "Tar (stones) row (knowing)" in Old Kingdom Cozen.

The 'modern' form involves ten cubes with five images and a blank side on each, usually carved of Sea worm bone. An older variant has only 40 images and thus two blank sides to each cube leaving out single images like Tempation, The lovers, etc. They are put in an Ovarwood cup (or leather in travel versions with an Ovar base), shaken and then spilled out on a cloth that has two interlocking circles that overlap for a small sector.

The position of the cubes in the sectors determine how the image influences the caster—

Hope Influences Duty

Past Obstacles Future

A single circle reading reads to the four points:

Obstacles Duty

Hope Outcome

Or

Needs Desires

Hopes Obstacles

With the circle cut in four.

The symbols on the cubes are:

1. The Priest—He is the path to the spirit using intellect, a positive cube, but with the caveat that to be caught up in the form of things can be misleading.

2. The Priestess—The path to the spirit using intuitive abilities but with the caveat that emotion must not overrule caution.

3. The Sacred Fool— The fool is the child hero/ine who experiences life in the moment and is ready for the world to amaze him/her. It can be a dangerous position to be in yet no fear accompanies this cube and he/she may go where the 'brave' will not and thus may gain greatness without really trying.

4. The Warp Wizard— a mysterious symbol that can mean control and change but also chaos and deception.

5. The Crystal Smith—fashions life from the lifeless, makes dreams come true and can, seemingly go against the natural order (but in fact, is part of it).

6. King of Blades—On a world of swords and knives blades are a necessity and signify both life and cunning. They are also utilitarian for many purposes and so this King is both an aggressive protector and worker, as positive sign. Or a destructive, cunning character. Also called the Saint of Blades.

7. Queen of Blades—this cube sign is indicative of the blade as a tool and constructive instrument of civilization.

8. King of Tankards—The Tankards are symbols of liquid emotions: positive and negative. The king is a carouser who can rage or love with great passion at the drop of a crown!

9. Queen of Tankards—Quick to love or hate the Queen of Tankards is a firey wench and a refined lady all at once.

10. King of Omphasts—is a marker of changes occurring, spiritually and physically. The king speaks of a positive change, even if not seen so at the time.

11. Queen of Omphasts—The Queen marks a change in a negative way, again, not necessarily viewed as such at the time.

12. King of Crystals—Master of living energy, he can send light, illuminate, or command a crystal weapon—indestructable and powerful but governed by strict laws. This is the cube of great power but with great responsibility.

13. Queen of Crystals—living Crystal is a major factor on Altiva- it embodies energy and light and life- it can bestow many gifts. The Queen is the major life giver of all the cubes.

14. King of Lanterns—Light and heat are positive but also the flame can

be dangerous. Unlike Glowgems this light can hurt and so there must be caution.

15. Queen of Lanterns—Here the fire of the Lantern signifies wholesome heat and illuminating a problem, but still with some caution to be observed.

16. The Z'last—The shadowstorm of the Cozen coast it can strip the flesh from a body in seconds: it signifies violent change.

17. The Twins— the two moons of Altiva have many phases, they provide light and guidance and though they seldom conjoin, this can occur and it is a celebrated and positive experience.

18. The Twins—the only cube sign that duplicates.

19. The Brothers—the two suns follow one after the other, The Elder being wise and leading the Younger Brother through the day sky. This signifies the need for or the actuality of guidance.

20. The Bandits—Sudden accumulation of wealth, often in a flashy or bold way; it can be spiritual wealth or gain as well.

21. The Manor House—Seen in the cube this once stable structure is a flame perhaps from external attack or from disaster within, either way it signifies that change, drastic and disruptive has or is about to occur. It can be good change or bad, however, depending on other factors.

22. The Vorn—A sign of reliability or skiddishness, depending on the position of the cube.

23. The Kota— The sign of communication and connection.

24. The Firehawk—A good luck symbol with a price; the Firehawk can consume all around it and sometimes itself in pursuit of its goals.

25. The Svor—a heard animal it is docile and content to take things slowly but can be a powerful force in groups.

26. The Tvek—a pack animal it is fierce and loyal, a little wild and dangerously aggressive.

27. The Warp—a sign of transformation in life, of going from one state to another rapidly.

28. The Gods—Not specific deities but the idea that outside forces control your destiny and you may have to sacrifice to them to progress.

29. Fierceness—This is not a violent aggression but rather a fierce devotion

to a cause of reaching a desired goal.

30. The Senses—As there are six senses so may this cube be a sign of forces overwhelming or en wrapping the caster/ee. It is easy to be confused by too much information and this Cube indicates the need to focus.

31. The Ensnared—The victim entrapped or ensnared is one kept from moving forward or back, stuck in one place until something or someone intervenes.

32. Transition This cube face of death also is a symbol of growth, of transitioning to a new level.

33. The Healer is dedicated to health but conversely can be harbinger of sickness or ill 'thought."

34. The Singer—a song can heal, bring joy or elicit strong emotions and this image represents many possibilities and great promise.

35. The Swordswoman—she is prepared to fight for what is right with skill and cunning. She is seldom defensive unless it is part of a deeper strategy.

36. The Contract House—the brothel is home to sacred union and symbolizes obligations and duties joyfully done.

37. The Beggar—unlike charity this is a cube of want, not need. It may not be so clear to the caster but it must make the questioner ask: what is needed and what is wanted?

38. The Sage—this fatherly figure can have wisdom or dogma to convey and his 'advice' must be carefully sifted.

39. The Child –is an innocent, but unlike the sacred fool needs to be guided and could be in great danger.

40. The Fansav—These demons of the Kovar Religion agitate for the status quo; they do not like change and enjoy to be in conjunction with the ensnared cube.

41. The Dreamspeaker –This Z'n dream interpreter is the conduit to the messages sent to mankind by the Gods and understanding the messages is vital to well being.

42. The Windmother—A fierce protector she can also be a stern taskmistress.

43. Temptation—What we do not have we often want. Is it good for us, or needed? It is our ability to resist that is a sign of strength.

44. The Lovers—The opposites who join in mutual sharing representing the fullfilment of life's missions.

45. Burdens—Both given and taken on, these can be obligations or inherited troubles all of which MUST be dealt with.

46. Charity—to give is to receive and this cube indicates the need to share the positive in order to receive the joy the world has to offer.

47. Loyalty—This can be to a person, idea or cause. It can be dangerous or over zealous loyalty and this can be a detriment if not carefully watched for.

48. Enemies—Real or imagined.

49. Friends—real or imagined.

50. Dangers—real or imagined.

ABOUT OUR CREATORS

WRITER

Teel James Glenn's poetry and short stories have been printed in over two hundred magazines including Weird Tales, Mystery Weekly, Pulp Adventures, Space & Time, Mad, Cirsova, Silverblade, and Sherlock Holmes Mystery.

His short story "The Clockwork Nutcracker" won best steampunk story for 2013 from Preditor and Editors poll. His novel A Cowboy in Carpathia: A Bob Howard Adventure won best novel 2021 in the Pulp Factory Award. He is also the winner of the 2012 Pulp Ark Award for Best Author.And was a finalist for the Derringer short mystery award in 2022.

His website is: TheUrbanSwashbuckler.com

INTERIOR ILLUSTRATIONS -

CHRIS NYE - has been a graphic artist and illustrator for over 30 years. He has actively worked in the comic book and graphic novel industry since 2001. In addition to work for Airship 27 Productions, he is currently working on comic book projects for Sitcomics and Markosia. He is also a graphic artist, illustrator and writer with Lockheed Martin. He resides in Simpsonville, South Carolina.

COVER ARTIST -

ROB DAVIS - began his professional art career doing illustrations for role-playing games in the late 1980's. Not long after he began lettering and inking, then penciling comics for a number of small black and white comics publishers- most notably for Eternity Comics, which eventually became Malibu Comics in the 1990's, on their book SCIMIDAR with writer R.A. Jones. Branching out to other black and white publishers and eventually working at both DC and Marvel Rob worked on likeness intensive comics like TV adaptations of QUANTUM LEAP and STAR TREK's many incarnations mostly on the DEEP SPACE NINE comics for Malibu. At Marvel he worked on the Saturday morning cartoon adaptation PIRATES OF DARK WATER. After the comics industry implosion in the late 1990's Rob picked up work on video games, advertising illustration and T-shirt design as well as some small press comics like ROBYN OF SHERWOOD for Caliber. Rob continues to do the odd self-published comic book as well as publisher and designer for his small-press production REDBUD STUDIO COMICS. Rob is Art Director, Designer and Illustrator for the New Pulp production outfit AIRSHIP 27 partnered with writer/editor Ron Fortier. Rob is the recipient of the PULP FACTORY AWARD for "Best Interior Illustrations" in 2010 for his work on SHERLOCK HOLMES: CONSULTING DETECTIVE and has been nominated for the same award every year since. He works and lives in central Missouri with his wife and two children.

THE WARP ORPHAN RETURNS

Vietnam veteran T.K. Mitchell never thought of himself as anything other than a former grunt doing his best to get by from day to day. Life was boringly routine until the appearance of an old woman calling herself Meegana Kakdon claiming to be a Warp Wizard.

She informs T.K. that he was actually born on another world called Altiva located in a different dimension than ours. A world in which his parents ruled. But traitorous foes plotted to overthrow them and before their deaths, they sent their baby to Earth. Now the time has come for T.K. to return to Altiva and claim his birthright.

In the blink of an eye, and very much against his will, T.K. is warped into a strange alien landscape with two suns, one red and one blue. Soon he encounters a warrior priest known as the Reverent Lord Enrique, the Shoutte of the Shoutte. Realizing the young man is a warp orphan, the cleric decides to be his guide. Day by day, T.K. begrudgingly comes to admire this strange and exotic world. A world filled with both beauty and danger to included the Royal Usurper who will stop at nothing to find and destroy him.

DRAGONTHROAT
—A NOVEL OF ALTIVA—

TEEL JAMES GLENN

TWICE THE DANGER

Jon Shadows, son of a fabled adventurer and mysterious female ninja assassin, courts danger wherever he goes.

In volume one Jon Shadows is a freelance bodyguard and investigator. When his ex-lover, Maria, tells him her billionaire husband, William Carter, is trying to kill her, he can't help but come to her aid. Shadows' plan is to attend an annual corporate employee meeting on Carter's private island and do some digging.

He soon discovers the eccentric computer mogul has ominous ties to the Japanese crime syndicate known as the Yukaza and is already being investigated by the Securities and Exchange Commission. But before Shadows can make sense of the data, a close friend is brutally murdered and it looks like he is slated to be the killer's next target.

In volume two while visiting the alluring Flora Temple in New Orleans, a random act of violence leads them into a tangle of murder, robbery and more. Next, he is contacted by the widow of a former Marine buddy who suspects her husband's death was orchestrated by a billionaire genius sequestered on Wolf Island, a bizarre medieval fortress built on a remote island.

Award winning writer Teel James Glenn offers up double the thrills and derring-do synonymous with the one and only Jon Shadows.